First and Foremost I want to thank God for my Creativity!! And I want to thank my family and friends who have supported me along the way!!

Chapter 1

As I gazed solemnly around my room the Vera Wang bed which I totally loved, everything was adorned with pink from the softness of pink to deepest of my favorite color from my fluffy comforter to the memory foam pillows that were draped I thought were ever made or so I mind led me to believe I had stacked neatly upon my bed smiling gently to myself my fingers briskly touched the pink quilt that my Mom had made with such love and care even my pajamas and well-worn rabbit ears house slippers my feet seem to have a mind of its own always seeking them out. Glancing around my room we all had a thing for sticky notes they were placed all over the room my little sister Susan was a premature baby there was no one on this earth I loved more, a pain gripped my heart who was big on hearts telling me that she loved me some with only just that a heart I saved them all, several from my mom wishing me well on and exam or some other matter are her words of encouragement words that would remain with me forever more. Last but certainly not least my build a bear workshop collection I had amassed a very large collection babies as I liked to call them in every shape, and color and let's not forget my unicorn stage each one was dressed in the height of fashion laughing almost outright Briana was my first one I had acquired, I clutched her in my arms many a night so lost in my despair and fear with absolutely no one to turn to Briana had been my confidante of sorts I had told her all of my secrets gazing deep into those blue eyes of hers knowing in my heart she was not real all those dark and lonely nights she had been my one and only true friend. I treated each one like they were a member of my family, thanked them for all the love and comfort they had given me, kissed Briana quickly and placed her back on the bed upon my pillow Shaking my head sadly to myself, I shrugged my shoulders aggressively abruptly standing to my feet.

Walking over I opened the door to my walk in closet mom had always made sure we had hordes of clothes so finding something to wear would not be a big problem they were hung by their colors so I looked to my right in the very back that's where all of my darkest ones from the royal blue to the browns and blacks and I picked through those and chose a black pair of jeans a long sleeve black thin hoodie this had been a well thought out plan down to the last detail. I had chosen black to match my mood. My mind was like night, the place where darkness lingered. Pulling off my clothes and putting them into the dirty clothes hamper, I never liked to leave a mess for anyone to have to clean up after me. I had written a list of last-minute details not wanting to forget anything it was bad enough that I was going through with this but one thing I knew I needed to turn out right. I dressed in front of my long mirror attached to the back of my bedroom door, I slumped down on the edge of the bed pulling my socks on my feet, on the other side of me was my new sneakers a pink pair of Adidas but for the life of me, I didn't want them on my feet thinking it would be better if I left them off leaning over my bed. I grabbed my list. The next item had been very hard to do the hardest of them all but I had finally finished both of them late last night. The letters I had penned to my Mom and Susan and I had placed them both on my desk next to my computer. No matter I must get on with it, squatting down I reached under the bed and pulled out a box that I had ordered online from a hardware store it had been delivered only two days ago after receiving it I felt an urgency in me not wanting anything to derail me. I sat on the floor with the box and crossed my legs my nerves were on edge yanking open the box staring at the contents a sense of relief swirled around inside of me It was still there .....I glanced down at the rope like it was an old friend but old friend it was not merely being and means to an end there was such irony in that statement. I grabbed the chair roughly and centered it in the middle of the room glancing up at the ceiling. The house was modern by today's standards with a cabin feel each room had a single round long beam that was centered in the middle. I threw the rope over the beam it was rather heavy much heavier than it looked, making a noose while standing on the surface of the chair I sliding my head in the center of the noose, I tightened the rope around my neck my hands dropped down to my sides the sound pounding in my ears. I paused taking a deep breath, I had thought long and hard for some time about killing myself. My mind briefly drifted away thinking of those who would be affected by such a drastic decision. My Mom had raised us a with a firm belief in God, instilling in us what was right and what was wrong even though she had failed me so many times My Mom, My Sister, and my one and only friend April, we had often talked about us doing this simultaneously but being the bright star that she was the world could not afford to lose her it would definitely be a dark place if it did. No, this is something I must do alone and alone I must do it. Well I am small in stature, 110 pounds, this should be over very quickly, and I had done my research! I exhaled. Let's get on with this tedious task. I leaned to my right side in an attempt to knock my chair over, my chair went backwards from that very moment everything went in slow motion! Once the chair was no longer supporting my legs the rope slowly tightened to the point of not being able to breathe my body swayed back and forth, my muscles seemed to get into each other I gasped, because I felt a serve pressure building behind my eyes, my eyes bulged to the point I felt they would pop out my legs started to tremble violently ,there was an immense flame that was running up and down my spine had never felt such heat, I had used the bathroom minutes ago I had seen too many movies, not wanting my body waste to be everywhere for my Mom to have to clean up.It was going to be very hard on her as it was. Whoever said when you hang yourself you go instantly is a bold-faced lie. It wasn't like I was going to be able to come back and tell anyone no this was like the ultimate scenario. So before you think of this weigh all of my options , my life is slowly ebbing away, my mind is swirling in pain rejection and defeat, Not one to give up easily even in death But for the life of me I cannot even accomplish that life is playing a cruel joke on me. Over in the corner of the room I saw a bright light. The more I focused on the light it started to take shape out of the light and stepped an Angel, the Angel had a golden breastplate and gold cuff at his wrists he was utterly beautiful with a very shiny countenance.

It is true you were born, and you will one day die but today is not that day said the Angel, from the look in his eyes I knew that what I was attempting wasn't being received well. He glanced up at the beam that was supporting me. The rope around my neck loosened much needed air rushed into my lungs. I knew I was being supported while my body was placed prone on the floor. The knowledge suddenly filled my mind that he was my guardian Angel! Realizing at that exact second that I didn't want to die, and I laid there with the rope burns around my neck silently thanking God for giving me another chance. What led up to this moment in time? Are you asking yourself that? And I hope you are ,if time permits I will bring you up to speed, grab a seat. This may take a while. From the moment of my birth I was loved and cherished by both my parents, but then everything changed when my dad passed away when I was eight years old but I remember him vividly. My little sister was much younger than I so I can imagine that it must have been very hard on our Mom, our Grandmother and Grandfather would help out at intervals and we always stayed every summer with them but that was before my grandfather died I recall Grand that what we call her had grievously taken it very hard to quite honest we all had But Grand had stepped into her place as the family Matriarch and nothing had stopped her since , Mom was a nurse and her job was very important to her and to this day it still is not much has changed in that department She worked at Memorial Hermann was of the most prestigious hospitals in Houston. Normally working 12-hour shifts so she worked a lot often logging in a lot of overtime hours. Stability was the key in my mother's mind. Trust me I understand she was so used to my dad and what he brought to the table but trust me every man is not like my dad. We were soon to find out how true that statement was!

Chapter 2

Of course, it was only a matter of time before she remarried. I remember the first time I saw Chris he was tall, well-muscled a brunette with green eyes I could see why Mom found herself attracted to him, She often was heard saying to her friends how lucky she was to have met him, and how surprised she was he even noticed her I believe that's when her self-esteem started to slip maybe she wasn't good enough for him My aunt Julie overheard her and immediately said, No, he is extremely lucky to have you.   Do you know you're beautiful and the kindest person I know? I know my mom replied going on to name off all his good qualities once again making one think she wasn't good enough for him and I could not fathom the reason behind her feeling this way. Susan was swayed early on it took me sometime to begin to trust him, Mom asked me to be nice to him when she talked about him her eyes took on a dreamy look her face softened she glowed and I had to admit it was due to Chris he turned out to be a sweet, kind, loving step-father always fun he wanted to spend time with my sister and I not knowing he was grooming us for him after their big glitzy overpriced wedding that my mom paid for mind you, We settled into a family of sorts, but what looks good on the outside does not mean it is good on the inside.   Chris and Mom both worked and we went to school, Mom was big on cooking family meals and keeping the house clean Susan and I helped as much as we could when we became old enough Mom had assigned us chores Susan and I both liked it because we looked at it like it was a game so that made it fun some nights Mom came in from work with rings around her eyes and stress on her face she tried to hide it from me But I began to notice that something was off about her going from a fun loving person, bubbly with loads of energy to border line withdrawn we somehow felt that it was our fault we sought her out whenever she was

home she came out of her room and sit on the couch after preparing dinner and just stare

off into space leaving the care of us into Chris's hands his habits started to change he would

come in late at night and they would argue for hours on end walking around on pins and

needles was our forte.   I called Grand, she came over and cooked and we helped her keep

the house neat. The only thing Mom had any interest in was working. She continued to go

but everything else she let go. Her appearance suffered greatly. She wore her robe and an

alternate house dress. Her hair was in disarray, not giving a care for how she looked, what

was happening to our happy life? Our close-knit family was coming unhinged right before

our very eyes and there was little to nothing that they could do about it. During the periods

of fighting and name calling Chris would cook and try to bring order to our meager

existence, clothes went unwashed, Grand taught me how to wash and cook several

nutritious meals between us we kept the house going. Growing older I became aware of

several things the tension in the house became insurmountable and if Mom and Chris once

loved one another I think that emotion has long since been taken off the table! Always felt I

needed to support my Mom. That's what families are supposed to do. If Susan and I hang in

there with Mom maybe she would come out of the slump, she is in. Grand called over both

my aunts and they had an impromptu meeting about our state of affairs. I walked in on

them having a very heated argument about Mom's mental state, realizing that they blamed

Chris, for everything that she was going through, Grand was adamant about finding a way

to get rid of Chris, we all knew he wouldn't go quietly, if they had taken that initiative and

that course of action then maybe we would not have become his victims. Talking long into

the night Grand wanted to remove us from our home moving us into her house she had plenty of room. Both my aunts strongly disagree with her; this may be the final straw to tip the scales in my mother's mind that could place her in total chaos.   Grand finally coming to the conclusion to take us for a couple of days to seemly clear the air this was a drastic decision Grand said, maybe this is what she needs to jump start her thought pattern when she realizes we are gone being front and center of the melee I seriously doubted any of their plans would help in shape form or fashion. Susan and I went in to pack a small bag for each of us, they went in to tell my Mom and Chris she stepped back and blinked rapidly like her mind was in a fog, Chris pulled her roughly to him and glanced down at her and smiled a smile but it didn't quite reach his eyes and said, Yes that's what we need, some alone time. Don't you agree dear? He asked my Mom if she looked around the room, her eyes resting on us and said quietly I guess so.   There was something ....in my Mom's eyes it sent a chill down my spine you must understand the nature of a thing recognizing it for what it was FEAR....she walked over and took a seat by the window, Chris continued to talk, Grand noticed what I was about to do and stepped up to engage Chris in conversation I joined my Mom I kneeled down near her and whispered Mom are you sure? She smiled meekly up at Chris and they made eye contact intently as if they had an unspoken language that only they understood. She reached out for Susan and me and held us to her bosom before momentarily closing her eyes he walked over and clasped her hands she was holding on tightly searching for a solace that was never to be found. Grand told us we would leave in the morning. I could tell she was worried about her daughter. None of us had ever seen her so distraught and disheveled, not knowing what I could do to help her, but I wanted to with all my heart! There was something we were missing it being so close we nearly could touch it, We all told Mom we loved her we hugged and kissed her I tried to relay some of my strength to her Aunt Julie rushed out the door with our bags my pulse starts racing my Grand tucks each of our hands in hers Mom shoves us abruptly to the door and said Go, Go, I will see you guys soon, I love you in an effort to get us gone as promptly as possible, Susan shook silently in the back seat next to me I held her in my arms Grand turned around and said, girls I know it doesn't seem like it now but it will get better while smiling gently at us. The ride to Grand's house was long and bleak or so it felt to me truthfully all I felt was relief like a burden had been lifted from my soul and spirit. Susan slumped against me. I told her we were embarking on a great adventure from past experiences we knew would indeed be that. Glancing down into her eyes they were small in her very timid face, but they were shining brightly with the love that I glimpsed there. I smirked and placed my head on top of hers. Suddenly the tires crunched on the gravel as we pulled up into her driveway. Grand said, girls were home gathering all our things and we proceeded to the front door. We went in the house headed straight for our bedroom it was beautiful Grand had the décor a mixture of pink for me and yellow for Susan she was awesome indeed always thinking about us, Susan I said before she reminds us let's put away our clothes sometime later she called us into the Kitchen the smells tinged our noses when we opened the door homemade cookies and popcorn balls Grand knew those were our favorites. Susan jumped up and down, Oh Grand we love you, and Grand blushed and grabbed a paper towel and wiped her hands before hugging us both. Aunt Sophie had fried chicken and she made mashed potatoes and green beans. Kimberly put the food on serving platters and Susan set the table. She didn't have to tell us twice Grand placed a pitcher of fresh milk and juice on the table. Grand sat at the head of the table. I was on her left with Aunt Julie and Susan was on the right with Aunt Sophie. We bowed our heads while Grand said the blessing. Susan was beaming to see the happiness in her made me ecstatic we laughed and talked amongst ourselves it was one of best meals we had as a family. Suddenly thinking of Mom wishing she was here with us. Ok Girls got the kitchen tidy because this is movie night .Grand said We jumped up and hurried as fast as we could washing the dishes and putting them into the cabinets with the speed of the Flash himself.

Aunt Julie and Aunt Sophie placed a tablecloth on the coffee table, Grand now don't you forget to put towels on the floor in case you guys make a mess you know I usually don't allow anyone to eat in the living room but tonight is a special occasion said Grand we all smiled at her in return Aunt Julie was busy arranging the enormous popcorn balls and the chocolate chip cookie which were sporting some big chocolate chunks.

Chapter 3

Susan eyes grew large in wonder adding to the feast big mugs of ice cold milk that was frosty on the top With a twinkle in her eye Grand took her seat with such grandeur only a queen such as herself could pull off, We had been playing this game since we were babies Grand should have been born in times past her heart longed for when the kings and queens ruled the land we listened attentive as Grand wove a tale of love and rich splendor the title gentlemen and gentlewomen meant a lot love wasn't just a word to say but a feeling to be felt. We ate until our tummies were full; no one on God's green earth made us feel as grand did, not even Mom. A sadness tugged at my heart noticing me and Grand said, no time for feeling melancholy, a frown is an upside-down smile so turn it around smiling widely at her so she wouldn't worry about me!   Susan ran over to Grand with her fingers in curls deciding to join her, we ventured, off into one of our tickle fights we tickled Grand she was laying spent in the middle of the floor

and we asked her, Grandma have you had enough? She squeaked Yes and I got your Grandma not liking to be called grandma at all so we would say it sometimes to tease her rolling over and standing to her feet she said you guys are going to be the death of me. Aunt Julie and Sophie had been watching one of the movies both said Mom you are so dramatic. She answered sure I am! What a mess! She said in an exasperated tone we immediately started cleaning, we were moving at such a high rate of speed I was dizzy, we stood back and we looked at our work, we had completely put the room back in order next time you will get a chance to watch the movies I promise. Kimberly and Susan its bath time we kissed her and ran off down the hall to our room after that daunting task Aunt Julie came in to tuck us in Aunt Sophie had gone home she was so quiet you hardly knew she was here but anyway she tucked us into bed after we had said prayers she kissed us on our foreheads finally leaving us alone we had had a very long day and personally I was glad it was over she shut the door and went into the living room with Grand she was singing softly to herself she went into her room aunt Julie retrieved a glass of tea and went into hers Grand had an opened door policy at night in case we were in need of her we knew we could go to Grand she always made us feel loved and cherished. Shortly before we had come to Grand's house Susan had started having nightmares I felt it was because of all the tension in the house, Of course Mom had never taken responsibility for that she had blamed it on Horror movies but she and I knew that wasn't the case Because she stopped that eons ago, and I had stopped also because Susan was too delicate for that But if our Mom had paid close attention to us at all she would of known that from the other bed I heard my sister softly snoring I sighed in relief peace settled over me as I drifted off to sleep.

Today was Saturday realizing that when I heard pots and pans clanged together Grand was cooking us one of her world-famous Breakfast's We quickly washed our faces and brushed our teeth there was a platter on the counter with Bacon, and Banana nut pancakes. Do you girls want grits we both declined, she said well it's too late I already have a small pot on the stove. Set the table girls Grand said I'm not as strong as I used to be, I stared at Grand nervously just in time to catch her winking at me over Susan's head I winked back. Susan and I both needed to feel useful singing our happy song a song Grand had invented to make our meals more delightful it always brought a huge smile to our faces we gathered around the table we clasped our hands together and bowed our heads and thank the all mighty God for all his blessings and for the food we were about to eat. Grand's pancakes were yummy with pecans and lots of syrup with bacon and a small dollop of grits on the side for a meal! We both looked our plates over, how could we eat it all? I thought happily to myself no matter the fun was in trying to master it. Susan grinned at me while stuffing her mouth who said she couldn't do two things at once. I said to her Good she said UN huh. Unable to form the words around the pancakes we ate in silence for several minutes Grand jumped up and retrieved the milk you girls must drink milk I rolled my eyes we want strong healthy girls right and bumped into me after noticing my frown. I said yes ma'am she said you don't have to say ma'am to me I'm not and old fuddle dud die Aunt Julie said we know Mom with a smirk upon her face a thought quickly raced across my mind that these are moments in one's life that memories are made of this is what we were lacking in lately in our lives but leave it to Grand to bring it back. Run along girls get yourselves tidy and get dressed Julie will take care of the kitchen for today.I stopped and turned around and said Are you sure? They both answered in unison yes, we are, I pressed the on button for the game we got lost in the game for several hours until Aunt Julie called us and told us we were leaving so get ready and we did. Grand and Aunt Julie took us to the park one of the biggest in the area we ran and played until we were in a state of blissful exhaustion we had a picnic under one of the massive oak trees Susan and I placed a blanket out Grand and Aunt Julie spread out sandwiches, fruit, and plate of fresh veggies with juice to wash it all down. Susan and I laid back and looked up at the sky. We gave Grand read one of her many novels and Aunt Julie walked away talking quietly on her phone. Susan started to point to the clouds naming them I joined in not wanting to be left out of the fun.   Noticing the family in our vicinity Grand not ever meeting a stranger introduced us all to them Mr. and Mrs. Palmers they had three children two girls Anna and Helen and one son David the girls were around our age all of their faces were glued to the phone with an extreme concentration written on their faces Susan suddenly hey we came to park let's play they placed their phone on the blanket beside Grand she handed out our stuff I didn't realize Grand had bought all of this am glad she did we had a bag with bubbles David showing us how to make bubble bombs next Frisbees and badminton after seeing our fare David brightened up immediately. Aunt Julie took us over to the tennis courts and divided us into Sisters. She called them, and she and David played together passing the rackets out and the birdies we played for sometimes, Grand was sitting there laughing at our antics . After a long while the Palmers called their over saying it was time to leave we hugged each other Anna and her siblings said they hadn't that much fun in ages We hugged briefly promising to keep in touch we all sometimes say that but this I hope we did. Grand hearing her said, in the world of high technology sometimes it is a relief to get back to the business of just having plain fun. The parents didn't say anything. I smiled sadly at them, not once did they put down their phone. But we children totally understood what she was referring to, Because had just lived the prime example before they left Anna ran over to Grand and gave her a hug and told her in a small voice you are awesome. Grand hugged her back and said Why thank you child. She ran back to join her family as they hurried off to their car before getting in, I glimpsed a look of longing in her eyes. We had exchanged numbers with David commenting you must have a land line I said yes we do it a little embarrassed I said it is so stone age handing her my number I said use it don't lose it she smirked at me we were given their numbers I glanced at her in surprise because I had never made a friend so easily Smiling to myself thinking of my Grandma no one had to tell us of the treasure that we had in Grand, because she was a true treasure indeed. Just those words made me appreciate Grand all the more.

Ok Girls Aunt Julie said, Let's gather our things and it's time for us to hit the road jack and we all burst out laughing. My, how time flies when you have not a care in the world. Piling into the car listening to Grand constant chattering Susan held my hand I closed my eyes for mere second when people say they don't know what peace is well I do I may not be old by society's standards But thanks to my loving family I know what peace is and I found that I liked it very much!

Chapter 4

Stopping at the supermarket to retrieve a few items one being ice cream to go along with our dinner Grand had opted out to invest in cable she chose to rent various movies so since we missed the movies from last night she decided to lets us make up for it tonight we stopped at the Redbox kiosk Grand and Aunt Julie agreed on a love story and we chose Chap pie and Fast and furious 8 fast cars and hot girls and independent females what's not to like, Susan wanting the former she said oh please Kimberly I been wanting to see this movie for such a long time, I ruffled her hair and said ok kiddo. Retrieving the movies, I listened half-heartedly while Grand gave us all a live trailer of her movie. Aunt Julie said, we must get home before the ice cream melts mom, Grand you are right so you can drive Julie giving her the keys Susan and I both smirked because we knew Grand hated to be rushed. Pulling up in front of the Grand house we noticed a familiar car, it was Chris's car. For some earthly reason fear gripped me.I calmed myself out of the corner of my eye. I could see Susan's eyes focused on me. Suddenly, Chris jumped out of the car before we even had our doors opened and beckoned for my Mom to get out and join him. The sun was setting on the horizon. I guess that's why I found it strange for my mother to be sporting a pair of wide rimmed very dark sunglasses, her skin looked shallow and gaunt, Susan screamed Mom, I missed you so very much! With Grandma and Aunt Julie and I coming up the rear we all met in the center of her yard. Chris smelled of alcohol and staggered slightly Hello girls, Chris said He regarded us with a menacing gleam in his eyes he quickly masked it. I stepped back. I feared I was the only one that saw him for what he truly was. He said Angela couldn't sleep without you guys that's why she is wearing the sunglasses her eyes are very tired. From the look on everyone's faces no one I could tell believed him. Grabbing Mom roughly by her arm she flinched in pain, that's when I noticed several dark bruises on her upper arms underneath her light-colored blouse it was very sheer and not to Mom's taste at all. My Mom said in a very shaky voice Chris you were the one who wanted to come for the girls. He stepped in front of her, but we visibly saw my Mother shrunk. She was shaking before our eyes from his presence acting like we were unaware of this. Grand said Chris was just going inside for dinner, but we knew the invitation did not include him. But he had been drinking so his senses were lacking, and a bit slow Grand was as smart as a whip and I don't think he could fathom how cunning she really was. But Chris wasn't genuinely up to par and we all knew that. He started laughing really silly. Glancing down at my Mom he muttered a home cooked meal would really be nice we haven't had one in a long time because Angela you're cooking isn't fit for pigs. Grand gasped Why Chris, that is not nice! She said. Mom stepped back like she had been struck by his harsh words. Grand told us gently to go to our room and we went into the house, I placed the ice cream into the freezer, we both bolted down the hall, I left the door slightly ajar. While Grand dealt with them and dealt with she did! No, I resent that invitation for dinner, you both need to go get cleaned up and she looked directly at Chris and said you need to get sober you have a family to take care of. Chris stepped quickly up to my Grandmother and I heard him say Shut up old lady and mind your own business. Grand dropped her purse and she pulled out a 357 handgun, I heard the bolt slip into place when she turned the safety off and aimed the gun straight at Chris. Mom screamed, she started to wail hysterically. I was astonished when Grand started carrying? I heard Aunt Julie say you guys need to get in your car and leave Chris stumbled yanking the door open to the car Screaming at my mom Angela get your ass into the car. My mom hung her head and scooted over and shut her door. And Angela you can't have the girls back until you are in better shape Grand said! Do you hear me? I heard my mom say yes, But Chris's voice changed from slurred to threatening once he got behind the wheel. He said, Old lady, you're going to regret this, you can't keep our children from us. They took off with a loud squeak of the tires and gravel flying everywhere Grand came into the house her body sagged against the counter her face ghastly pale we assisted her to the couch and gave her something to drink Grand said go into my room bring me my grey little bottle I ran into her room and came back and I opened it and placed one of the pills under her tongue as was customary for her to do. Aunt Julie came out of the bathroom with her towel wrapped around her head! I took her in the kitchen and told her what had happened, she bit her lip nervously and said Mom are you alright? Grand answered and said Yes dear I feel so much better I apologize to you girls for all this ruckus lounging silently for some time she attempted to get up, I said Grand why don't we order pizza, Susan and I would love that, Aunt Julie interrupted and said it sounds good to me Mom! Grand grimaced and said, Pizza it is! We ordered from Pizza Hut and Aunt Julie went to retrieve it and I saw the worry in Grand's eyes. I decided a distraction was in order I put Chap pie in the DVD player once the nitroglycerin started to work Grandma's color returned to normal I went to the door to assist Aunt Julie she bought in three pizzas all of our favorites and we were elated we all went to the kitchen table and Grand instructed me to go into the pantry and she had Coca-Cola she had them for special occasions she reminded us that this was one of them she didn't allow us to have soda but we loved it anyway, I tapped Susan lightly on the arm and said you first, she responded no you, and this went for a minute more until Aunt Julie said Enough Dig in, and we did!One of the pizza was a deep dish pepperoni with cheese in the crust the cheese was so thick and gooey I closed my eyes and bit down into it, um um was all that I could say, Susan said this is heavenly and we all agreed yes it is we said. We plunged into the rest of the meal and devoured it in no time at all. Aunt Julie cleaned the dishes and kitchen area and escorted Grand into the living room and pushed play on the vcr the movie started, and we were soon engrossed right where we left off, Chappie taking us to another time and place tears flowed freely by the end of the movie. Grandma said, that really tugged at my heart's strings, Chappie was so human even more so than some of the people we have walking this earth today. I said, The Fast and the Furious who is with me? Yeah! Both Grand and Susan said, me! Me! Replacing the movie with as much fanfare as possible. Susan giggled and said Kim you're so funny! And arched an eyebrow and said, if only you knew! Noticing that Grand had grown quiet shadows fleeted across her face and she had very pensive look upon her face I sat back down near Grand and rested my hand on her arm and she glanced at Susan and Kim and Aunt Julie and said with a mixture of surprise and concern Her expression changed into a soft smile and she asked, Have I told you girls today that I love you? No matter what, always remember that! I said we will Grand! Page39. Grand said softly Movie please, our eyes met, and her head bobbed up and down. I realized that night I must step up and protect Susan, Grand and even Mom the movie started after it was over, I jumped up and said it certainly lived up to its name! it was awesome! The quiet was deafening glancing around and I saw that Grand and Susan were fast asleep, and I didn't even hear Aunt Julie when she retired to her room. The telephone rings as I proceeded down to the hallway with Susan in tow. There would be no baths tonight. I tucked her into bed kissing her lightly on her cheek, changing into my pj's. I could hear Grandma talking with persistence and the urge to go back into the living room with Grand to get a front seat to the conversation under the guise of being thirsty. No, I would let them have a private te te without any interruption from me.

Chapter 5

Sliding under the covers and I tried in vain to go to sleep, But I tossed and turned most of the night, I thought of my life, it was a puzzle. With jagged edges and the unsure piece at the center of my world was my Mom and somewhere all the way she had lost her self-worth and a way to help her get it back was the key I finally drifted off around 3:00am. Grand called us into breakfast around 8:00am, she was an early riser staggering out of the bed, rubbing my eyes, I made my way to the bathroom for that much needed shower I made it a quick one. When I walked in Grand said Kim dear, breakfast is ready, smiling I said yes ma'am. She said, don't say ma'am to me, I mimicked her and said I'm not and old fuddie duddie!Stop Kim, she said sit down and say grace it is your turn taking my seat I bowed my head and said, God can I eat my food? Everyone started to laugh but Grand said Kimberly I closed my eyes and thanked God for this hearty meal and for blessing my family when I opened my eyes Grand had a huge smile on her face but reprimanded me anyway by saying it's a time for joking and regrets and this one I regretted the most. We all piled into Aunt Julie's expedition it would accommodate us all with room to spare. Why is it when you are traveling somewhere you have no desire to go the distance is much quicker? A question I'm sure has been asked many times over the decades. We pulled up in front of the house the light was like a beacon, a welcoming one it was not. Susan jumped out of the car and ran to the front door; she was happy to be home. The familiar was what was important to her and even I knew that. It annoyed me that she was so elated, I must bury these feelings that I have, there was a fury that was building up inside of me, Susan saw good in everyone even Mom and Chris but that was wearing thin and I wouldn't allow them to hurt her. What they didn't realize is that Susan saw a lot more than they gave her credit for. Chris drunkenly came to the door; Susan ran into the house and both my aunts shouldered past him not even bothering to speak. Grand walked briskly into the house Angela, Angela where are you she asked? Mom ventured out of the bedroom wearing a long sleeve sweater and sunglasses on her face in the house. Grand asked, why are you so bundled up? Evading Grand's question she said, Kimberly and Susan I forgot you guys were coming home today. Julie and Sophie I wasn't expecting company! Aunt Julie and Aunt Sophie looked at each other and totally ignored her statement, Aunt Julie asked, have you ever heard that song I wear my sunglasses at night, So I can see! We all started laughing but the tension was so thick you could cut it with a knife. Grand leaned over and quickly snatched the glasses off my Mom's face, her face was swollen, and her eyes were blood shot red and rimmed in deep blue and purple bruises. Grand hand sprang to her mouth and she whispered, Oh Angela Baby, Aunt Julie said, Oh my God! Aunt Sophie asked, what happened to you? Susan and I started to cry I took her to the couch and we sat down and we held each other. Mom said, I fell at work! Not quite making eye contact with anyone. Grand asked, fell how? I called your job and they informed me that you had taken a thirty-day emergency leave. Mom sat down abruptly and said, Mom you shouldn't have done that! You had no right! Grand answered, I have no right, I have all the rights in the world you are my daughter, and I'll be damn if I will let this happen to you, Mom started silently crying, My Aunt's turned their attention to Chris he was sitting quietly in the kitchen fuming. Mom's sisters stood over him in a belligerent manner. and said Angela is black and blue, what do you have to say for yourself? Not a damn thing, he answered. They were so shocked they started to plummet him with their fists hitting him everywhere it was possible. She shouldn't be so clumsy! He jumped up yelling, You Bitches are all crazy! Grand walked up to him so fast it surprised me she pulled out her gun and said if you so much as ruffle a hair on her head I will come back here, clean house and you will be leaving in a body bag. Do you understand me? Chris put his hands on his hips and said, old lady you have overstayed your welcome and I want you out of my house this minute. Grand said, this is my daughters house you best to remember that, or you will be the one leaving. Chris said, Angela you'd better get them out of here as he walked by them and went into the bedroom and slammed the door. Grand said I'm assuming you're bruised all over that being the reasoning behind wearing a sweater in June! Angela, you need to get rid of him. He is not good enough for you. And that's a fact Mom said, but I love him, and you'll don't know or understand him. Julie and Sophie, What a croc! Aunt Julie said , he is a pompous ass that is full of himself that married a very good woman and mother and is threatened by how beautiful and smart that you are and more than likely is jealous of how close knit our family is. Chapter 5 Have you ever met any of his family? Have you? I'm more than sure there is a reason why and one not too favorable. I'm sure. Her sisters sat on either side of her holding and comforting her. Susan had fallen to sleep. I took her to her room and laid her down and then I went and sat at Mom's feet and rested my head in her lap before long everyone was in tears. Grand went into the kitchen tidying it up. She had a meal started in no time at all. I cleaned the living room and den while Grand and her daughters talked. I went into check on Susan she was fast asleep her way of retreating from all the chaos, she was afraid as loud as we had been I'm sure she had heard some of our conversation if not all of it placing two fingertips on my lips and then put my fingertips the bridge of her nose something I knew she hated, even in her sleep she frowned. Laughing quietly to myself I exited her room. The house smelled and looked like the home I so adored. In the small amount of time we had been there

surrounding her with love and support she was acting more like her old self. I heard

laughter and it was my Mom, my heart soared not realizing how hungry I was for her laugh

and her constant chatter. That had ceased so long ago he had tried to diminish the woman

that she was, and he had almost succeeded. I wanted them to stay but I knew that was

impossible, but a girl could dream, couldn't I? I skipped up to Grand, my Aunts, and My

Mom and hugged each and every one. Aunt Sophie said, Once an abuser is always an

abuser! Given Mom much to ponder, she was very deep in thought. Grand called us all into

dinner. The meal was hearty and delicious. Aunt Julie talked quietly with Mom, and Mom

shook her head and wrung her hands in a defeated manner. Everyone minus Mom kept a

good-hearted banner going for some time with Mom finally joining in. Mom's bedroom

door hinges made a squeaking sound when opened slowly, Chris obviously was unaware of

this, so we heard him and knew he was listening to us. Our mood rapidly turned from

happy and carefree to a somber tone. He strolled into the room freshly shaven dressed in

clean clothes with a smile pasted on his face, and said I see I'm in time for one of Momma's

delectable meals. Grand stood up and briskly walked over to Chris with her finger pointed

in his face, the gentle Grandma was gone and in her place was a fierce protector of her

family not even recognizing "Grandma" and the voice emanating from her was stern and

foreboding, she was a force to be reckoned with. All of the false bravado and cheerfulness

leaving Chris like a tire on the a car when it is deflated she said I'm no Mother of yours and

do not refer to me as such, look around you I'm theirs, He glanced at Mom and my Aunts

and me and Susan with a smile on his face that quickly turned into a sneer, he threw his

hands in the air. Grand continued you lost that chance Mr. we are family and you are an outsider to us now. There is no redemption for you. Angela has given you chance after chance you will never change, you always disappoint her, well no more, we will not stand for it. Chris' eyes grew large in his face cowering back against the refrigerator with his hands on the counter in order to steady himself. Glancing quickly at Mom I saw clarity in her eyes, like she was seeing Chris for the first time for who he truly was when confronted by a strong woman it narrowed him down to size. Grand stood strong fast like a warrior on the battlefield, a victor in so much chaos and turmoil. Everyone got up and stood at Grand's side. I grasped Grand's arm to lend my support. Chris cried as though he had been struck then said Angela, I love you, please forgive me, give me another chance? I promise this time it will be different. Tears ran unchecked down his face and all eyes settled on Mom, clearly you could see she was still very much in love with Chris, and she refused to give him up. Mom started to wail, her body was wracked with her sobs Susan and I ran to sit next to our Mother, as she silently cried Susan said, Mom we're here and we love you! Aunt Julie countered; we all do Angela! Aunt Sophie said and somehow, we will all get through this! Chris quickly stomped across the room, and yanked my mom up by her arm, screaming they're not taking you from me, do you understand me Angela he asked? Grandma placed her arm around my mother's shoulders and turned her back on Chris. Her hands began to tremble, and she wearily fell into a chair opposite us. She gestured toward the coffee pot, I quickly got to retrieve her a cup. Chris' watery eyes were fastened on my Grandma, He gasped and said, you never liked me, and don't try and deny it because I know it's true! My Grandma answered, No , I never have had a sinking feeling in the middle of my stomach the moment I met you, now I know my suspicions were true! Mom accepts the coffee with a grateful smile after taking several sips, she said Chris what do we do now? You have had several affairs since we have been married, we all glanced at each other in shock, normally he would be denying what was being said but not this time. Mom, tilted her head, her finger lightly tapping her cup before she burst forth with I don't trust you, and I doubt if I ever will! Chris started to pace back and forth with agitation. How can you say that Angela? Chris asked, Mom sat up straight in her chair and stared in his eyes and said, I cannot fathom what made you change from the loving man I married, you care only for yourself she said like a streaming locomotive racing down the tracks she was gathering steam we glimpsed the strong woman we knew my Mom to be, at this moment I was prouder of my Mom than I have ever been for she was standing up for herself regaling with tale after tale of his exploits we were all stupefied grabbing Susan by the hand I took her to my room. talking quietly to her she laid down on the bed I laid down with her lightly stroking her hair she whispered to me I will be glad when this is over! Kim do you think this will ever end? I whispered back glancing down into her eyes fatigue was mirrored there for me to see , shakily pasting a smile upon my face, yes it will you know Mom always one for the dramatic!Susan said un huh. Resting lightly against the headboard the noise coming from the other side of the door was reaching a crescendo. Mom, Julie please don't do this, Aunt Sophie said desperately. Aunt Julie said he deserves everything that he's got coming to him. Mom's voice was muffled, barely audible, you don't know him. He's had a very hard time in his life! Everyone deserves forgiveness, isn't that what you taught us Mom? She asked. Suddenly she said, He didn't have a positive role in his life. His thought pattern is all scrambled up, it's hard for him to differentiate between right and wrong! Why are you defending him, asked Aunt Julie? Because he is my husband, Mom said. Yes we all do make mistakes, but you are wrong he does know what he is doing he just doesn't care if you think he does you are sadly mistaken and you know it I ran back into the living room leaning against the wall too disturbed to sit down Mom's face paled which made the bruises more visible, Grand said I will report you to Children and Family Services if you do put the girls needs first. You can't possibly be serious Mom stated.

Chapter 6

Grand said, Yes, I am serious, he has you so twisted and backwards you seem to have forgotten that. I will get custody of the children and you will never get them back! They are confused and scared Angela! I thought I taught you better than this, this is not who you are! Mom held her head down shamefully as she realized she had been putting Chris first for some time now. Grand said, your life is like a circus and Chris is the clown, He veered his head from across the room glancing at her and pleaded please don't do this, you are all that I have! Grand said," I seriously doubt that!" Chris, we want you to pack your things and leave now Aunt Sophie said, Aunt Julie said, yes and get all your stuff because YOU'RE NOT COMING BACK, SHE SHOUTED! Chris came forward, his shoulders slouched all the fight had gone out of him; Angela is this what you want? Mom didn't say a word, answer me he said raising his voice he said with venom, you're such a bitch! Mom winced at his onslaught of harsh words to her, He ranted and raved for another five minutes. My mom suddenly hollered and said, I want a divorce! And I want my children there is no place for you here! He stooped down and got in my Mom's face and said, you will regret the day that you crossed me. He looked at all of us with menace, a spittle was settling at the corners of his mouth. He looked delusional. Actually, it was terrifying to see him in this state. Chris said, I knew you would betray me! It was only a matter of time! I saw my mother reaction to the words of her abuser, yes that what he was saying to her his words seemed to sink deep within her being, she looked like she was in a trance after Grand called her, she stared at her like it didn't register. Mom, stubble to her feet that's when we all noticed all down her legs were palm prints and at her ankles was strap marks, the severity of the abuse was open for all to see. Grand's eyes narrowed and she asked, Angela did he tie you down? I clenched my fists. I wanted to strike him so bad I didn't know what to do. My Mom evaded the question but said Mom you don't understand! Grand said, no dear you are the one that doesn't understand because I understand perfectly the nature of a beast, Mom looked so weary, but Grand wasn't backing off she would see this through to the very end. Aunt Sophie screamed, even now you are defending this fiend! I said excuse everyone around me in surprise I said calmly please don't disturb Susan she is sleeping. Grand said, we're sorry! Aunt Julie said, if I find out you have been submitting to the atrocities of this maniac, I will never speak to you again! Mom said, do as you wish! Why Mom I asked? Kimberly, she said, as her voice faded to a mere whisper. Chris, my mom said, I want you out of life and out of my house now and not a second longer will I put up with you. Mom said, I need not my family to tell me that the decision is mine and I've made it since you think I can't make up my mind. Angela! Chris exclaimed My Mom said Get out! Screaming at the top of her lungs, Mom never raised her voice, so I knew for now at least she had had enough! I will not lose my girls because of you, all of the women you have had call one of them. I'm sure one of them will come to your aid. Chris focused on all of their faces and finally said, You, know I have nowhere else to go. Grand said, Chris you should have thought of all of that before you did all of these horrible things to my daughter, while he was pleading his case Aunt Julie had quietly slipped from the room wondering what she was up to! but my thoughts strayed back to this whole scene that was unfolding right before my very eyes. Chris ran up to my Mom and dropped to his knees in her wake and Aunt Sophie said Oh the theatrics! My mother solemnly said, there is nothing more to be said, our marriage is over! She glanced away and closed her eyes. Did you hear her? Grand asked? Aunt Julie ran up to the group and dropped two large suitcases at his feet, here are your things Chris I even packed your toothbrush! Aunt Julie said with a finality that only she could have pulled off. Chris jumped to his feet and said I will always love you Angela answered, love yourself Chris, because I think if you did you would have never taken me through any of this! Grabbing his bags, he asked, did you put all of my things in here? No one commented, you could feel the resignation in the room he walked out without looking back leaving the front door wide open. I ran to the door slamming and locking it for fear he would come back. Leaning back against the door, breathing loudly unbeknownst to me, Susan had silently snuck up behind me and gave me the tightest hug, a hug that only someone that loved you could give. She said timidly, I'm so glad! I answered in return, I am too little one! We stayed locked in our embrace for several long minutes. Glancing back towards My Mom, they were all in a similar embrace everyone was in tears. The situation finally weighed on us all, we joined the others and Grand said, a group hug with big crocodile tears in her eyes. The relief was tremendous! I had come to realize that we are truly a loving family that depended on each other for support which was freely given, Mom said, much as I love all of this I have a kitchen to clean up and two antsy daughters that need baths and last but not least I have and appointment with the sandman. We all giggled and Grand interrupted us and said in her sweet but stern voice Angela was all staying the night Mom blushed and said, No you mustn't do that I appreciate the thought but.....Grand said, we decided this beforehand Mom beamed at her Mom looking grateful and happy. Grand said, I have put my affairs in order, and I will be here indefinitely spoken in that tone we all knew there would be no swaying her otherwise. Susan spun around in a ballet's twirl and said No mine's is better and I said no it's not my room is better than yours. Marching off down the hallway leaving the adults to be adults. We bathed in record time racing into our pajamas and we were in bed in no time at all. Let's have story time Susan agreeing with a smirk Yes let's! we told stories like we use too we talked long into the night before finally drifting off I saw Mom leaning over us kissing us both gently on our forehead and tucking us end I don't remember the last time she did that gesture I reached up and gave her a hug, I whispered I love you she said I love you girls too!

 Don't ever doubt that! Touching her nose something we all tended to do to the other she smiled and said Goodnight ladybug. Her nickname for me I hadn't heard in a very long time snuggled under the covers feeling safe and loved. Mom shut the doors so quietly I barely heard her before finally succumbing to sleep. The sunlight streamed through the windows; Susan was sitting up in bed playing her Nintendo game I said last one to wash up for breakfast is a rotten egg. Susan said back, na na I already beat you, I stuck out my tongue, and went into the bathroom and brushed my teeth and washed up as quickly as I could, Grand said in a loud voice, Girls Breakfast is ready and waiting for you hurry because I will not put up with your shenanigans we said, Yes ma'am!

Chapter 7

Grandma answered Don't ma'am me! Sounding displeased as we knew she would be, smiling to ourselves we dressed in pants and blouses Susan wanted to show off our new phones to our Mother but I told her I commented that this was our secret, and we had given our word to everyone and until we are entirely certain of our Mom this is one secret that we keep! I placed my fingers together and crossed them over each other lightly touching my fingers to Susan's fingers our signal that we solemnly swore to each other. A smell was assaulting my senses, come on lazy bones, Mom said, we have orange juice and milk and....sitting down at the table, I said, good morning Grand and Aunt Julie both said good morning! Aunt Sophie smiled in our direction and placed a heaping plate of pancakes and bacon in front Susan and I Grand added a small bowl of grits, Grand remarked, the grits will make healthy, strong and wise little girls with a smirk on her face, Susan said, you always say that Grandma, I jumped in showing a sign of unity, yes you do Grand, and we have no proof of that I personally believe it to be nothing more than a pile of mush. Laughter erupted across the table. We wrinkled our noses to demonstrate our distaste; I stuck my fork in a thick pancake brimming with syrup and shut out the conversation concerning the grits. Peace was flowing like waves coming from my Mom, she was smiling really smiling my heart sang with joy! I jumped up from the table and ran and hugged and kissed my Mom. I am telling you all of this because there were so many bad memories, but this is a heartfelt good one. So, you will know that I never lost faith in my Mom and never truly stop loving her. My Aunts were quite at the table texting their families I'm sure. Everyone commenced eating, there was a need for further words! We all finished with full stomachs,

Grand was so proud, the light was shining in her eyes. Grand stood up and said, I've had

enough excitement to last me a lifetime she turned around and walked slowly over the

couch sinking gently down on it, we all knew she was very weary, Mom are you alright? all

her daughters asked her she leaned her head back against the couch cushions and closed

her eyes briefly. She chirped up and said, Girls I just need to lay down and rest for a few

minutes, ok Mom we understand, said my Mom She raised her fingers to her lips gestured

to us to be quite, Susan and I went into the kitchen to help with the breakfast clean up, we

started bumping and stumbling into each other grinning, before being shooed away to our

rooms. Grand opened her eyes suddenly and said yes, I am, I'm not a spring chicken

anymore closing her eyes once more I heard her when I went back into the living room to

check on her. Normally we would go outside in the morning, but Mom told us she didn't

want us outside without an adult Because of Chris and we were showing no resistance to

this. I glanced at Grand again I was worried about her, Grandma had never laid down

during the day, she always said, and idle mind is the devil's workshop we moved around

the house as quietly as we could not wanting to disturb her rest worry as etched on all of

our faces Susan drew pictures for Grand, and I read at least putting on the façade that I was

not absorbing one word that was on the pages. Aunt Julie and Aunt Sara were at the kitchen

table engrossed in a board game. Mom sat in her chair listening to her church hymns on her

recorded device. I could see the terror in her eyes, Grandma had stood up for her on more

than one occasion and if anything happened to Grand, she would blame herself? After

several hours of resting Grand woke up and said, why are you girls so quiet? I can hear my

own snores and that's not good chuckling to herself she got up off the couch in her own

confidante manner that she always held true to form, I am going to take a potty break, unless one of you want to hold my hand while I go we all glanced at her, she briskly walked into her room while we all laughter at her candor. Mom said, she certainly feels better and I thank God for that there was no denying that we all felt the same way. Grandma bounced back into the room with jubilance and said, I always did love a good board game, monopoly is it? Grand asked we all answered, yes ma'am she stopped and looked back at us and said her usual repetitive, don't say that to me, I'm not a ma'am she said with gales of laughter. Susan said in her small voice, Grand , I drew some pictures for you; Grand wiped her eyes and asked you did you? Come show me, Grand sat down in Mom's old brown wooden rocker that was also decked with several plush ivory pillows, Grand loved to sit there and she said it did wonders for her back. I jumped into action and made a steaming big bowl of popcorn while Mom made frothy ice cream shakes for everyone, I licked my lips thinking about them because they were legendary. Grandma, ooh! And aah over Susan's drawing. She said, you will be an artist one day! She asked, Grandma , do you think so?" Grand said, yes, I do dear kissing her on her cheek gently. Susan go put those in my room please, Susan turned and trustingly asked will my work be well received in the art world, her eyes bright with anticipation. We all said Yes Susan, she screamed and ran off to do Grand's bidding. Grand loudly said to Susan I do not wish to leave these you are building quite a portfolio. We joined my Aunt's at the table and the game began with grand coming away the victor. She chanted, don't look so forlorn girls Sugar Momma won! Mom said, we think you cheated Mom, Grand said, cheat no if you were a strategic, and clever as I am you would have won too. Boldly bragging, that sinking feeling you have in the center of your stomach is you're all eating crow. I snickered and handed over a dollar. That's what we had played for. She always wagged a dollar. She was indeed a smart woman. My Aunts pulled it out of their bras so for performance. Susan got up and pulled it out of hers, there were gasps all over the room she said with a smile I only did it because you guys always do. My Mom said ok, ok, enough already, Grand glanced at each of us and said, she is a chip off the old block ruffling our hair and bumping into me as she walked by Guys, let's have sandwiches for dinner because you been snacking all day, Aunt Sophie and Aunt Julie said, Yes a light meal would be nice. Sandwiches and chips, it is Grand said, Mom said, and we will fix it you rest this evening Grand started to protest but Mom was having none of it. Mom finally said, imagine all of the calories we have put on since we have all been under the same roof. They glanced at each other not quiet meeting her eyes that when I realized that is what they had planned to do all along to rally around Mom in her time of need, As Grand said with God at the forefront how could we go wrong that was an ingredient for a healthy life and I believed it to be so. I had wondered why my Aunts were still in attendance now I knew. Everyone was making a big effort to rebuild her strength, physically and emotionally, Mom seemed to be unaware of this and they were glad the plans were running smoothly, Grandma that school was starting soon, because of Mom's appearance I didn't want her embarrassed because of me she had enlisted my Aunt's to take us shopping, I stood and said glancing at the group I'm a fashionista and I don't want to disappoint the masses.

Chapter 8

Mom said, I could see sadness reflected in her eyes, I will take you honey, I responded if you feel better, I would love to go with you Mom. Grand interrupted and said, Angela you need time to recuperate and heal we will do this for you this one time ok? Mom shrugged her shoulders and said, ``Ok Mom , thank Julie and Sophie for your assistance. I can never repay you Aunt Sophie replied and said, just get well that's all we want sis. Sitting for our meal I silently thanked god for the best family ever. Aunt Sophie had her hand over her brow and said, here! Here! My how I wish this could last forever; we were rather wiped out our main concern being for Grand and my Mom. I kissed everyone and Susan and I followed Aunt Julie down the hallway she commented, if I stay up a moment longer you guys will have to hold my eyelids open with toothpicks, Susan and I glanced at each other and giggled as that image came to our minds, I heard Grand say, Yes let's call it a night, we all had a rather harrowing couple of days Mom said in a calm voice, yes we have Kim you Susan take your baths in the morning, brush your teeth and get into your pjs ok Mom I said, prodding Susan in the center her back to steer her into our room. I hear my Aunt's when they left but when I opened my eyes the silence was deafening I awoke Susan and we bathed and went into the kitchen Grand and Mom were sitting talking amongst themselves, I said Good Morning, Grand and Mom both answered good morning with Grand winking at us I winked back and grabbed a box of cereal out of the pantry and Mom handed us the milk Grand added girls I made you each a bowl of fruit after breakfast I kissed her and Grand on their cheeks Mom reminded me to take out the trash. I went outside dragging the trash barrel out to the curb, I suddenly felt a deep foreboding within my very being stopping dead in my tracks at the end of the driveway and the hairs rose on the back of my neck and arms. Suddenly feeling cold inside. Quickly glancing around I glimpsed Chris's car, my hands began to shake and my whole body trembled with fear, the passenger side window slowly slid down I heard Chris say, Kim come here baby girl I came here to see how you guys were getting along? I miss your Mom so very much; please tell her I am so incredibly sorry! I love you guys! My breathing was very rapid the tentacles of fear threatened to overcome me, I heard his car door open, Run my brain whispered to me I took off and ran with all my might, I was ashamed of myself for running not wanting Chris to see the fear had invoked in me I ran across the vast lawn not realizing until this very moment how big it really is! With Mom's array of flowers on full display but that thought was fleeting the slamming of the car door alerted me to the fact that Chris was fast approaching I couldn't allow him to catch up to me a sudden burst of speed aligned itself I could feel my adrenaline flowing to every cell in my body my legs moving so fast it didn't feel humanly possible but it was. I clutched the front door at that exact moment the doorknob was yanked open by my Grandmother I rushed past her. She felt my body shaking, taking me into her arms. She asked, What's wrong Kim? You look like you've seen a ghost. I slammed the door shut and locked it turning the key in the deadbolt to secure it. Gasping I was finding it hard to breathe mom came towards us! Chris, Chris I said Grand said, Chris what? he is out there! Just as I said that, there was a pounding at the door and the door bulged at the force of the pounding Angela, Angela let me in, you can't do this to me Susan ran out from the bedroom, surprise was written over all their faces, my Grandmother had obviously been expecting this to happen she pulled her purse to her from the other side of the counter and pulled her gun out she told us to step back. Chris was screeching and kicking the door, but Mom had the door replaced several years ago with one of the tops of the line titanium reinforced doors fearing a home invasion because there had been a spike of those types of crimes in our neighborhood in recent years! At the time I thought it was Mom being over the type and overprotective as usual, but now I thanked Mom on this insight with all the kicking and shoving the door held. Grand yelled and said, if you proceed, I will be shot and that's not a promise that's a fact. The pounding suddenly stopped, Mom sank down into her rocking chair with her hands over her ears she said over and over oh no! Oh no! too no one in particular retreating back into the world of pain and suffering! No, this could not be I ran over to the alarm panel he was attempting to raise the front windows feeling totally and utterly overwhelmed I pushed the panic button, the police would be alerted and a thought quickly raced through my mind concerning our neighbors most were at church during this time, so we are all alone in this! the minutes slowly dragged by about the Grand was at the door about to give up hope in the distance I could hear the distinct wail of police sirens, Chris hollered and said, you bitches called police! Seconds later we heard the car revving up and the squealing of the tires from Chris's departure, lights were flashing in front of our driveway from the patrol cars; Grand glanced out the window and said, Thank God! The next knock was a welcoming one; Grand opened the door slipping her gun into her apron pocket as she did at the watchful eyes of the officers. I turned off the panic button glad now that Mom had taught me how to operate it. The officers talked with my Mother after discovering she was injured and covered in bruises. they called an ambulance they checked the perimeter and the surrounding neighbors houses not being able to locate him they decided he had escaped APB was put on the airways for Chris Blackmon, Mom had calmed herself and answered all the questions that were put to her by the police without any hesitation. Susan stood at my side and held my hand with a strength I was unaware she possessed; they were diligent in their mannerisms and very competent. They informed my Mom that she must get a restraining order Chris. Because this indeed may keep him at bay, the ambulance arrived, and the paramedics escorted Mom out the stretcher and placed her into the back in order to examine her more privately.

I realized in that moment that they were true heroes, one of the officers approached us and gave us each a teddy bear, we thanked him tears were in Susan's eyes wanting to take her mind off what was happening I held my bear and said we must name them Susan's eyes brightened considerably she named her Maxie and I named mine Pinky, we sat on the corner of the couch while Grand explained to the officer the severity of the of Chris's behavior asking in turn if the restraining order would make a difference the shorter officer of the two commented ma'am it isn't a failsafe by any means, But if he does return and you must use force to stop him then you have informed the court that he is a danger you and your family and he enters your home without permission then you must protect yourself.

And Grand said, officer I do not wish to take a life because all life is precious but kill him. My daughter and granddaughter don't deserve this. No, ma'am they sure don't, he said. Pictures were taken of my Mom and she told the officers she would be at the courthouse at first light thanking the officers graciously both my Mom and Grand hugged each officer Also informing that a patrol car would periodically ride by our house during the night, we didn't know if it would stop Chris's rampage but we hoped it would. Okay ma'am please call us if you need us, Mom replied, we will! Leaving no doubt in our minds that she meant what she said, Before leaving the officer gave Mom a copy of the police report and Mom placed it upon the counter, which I read it was detailed and precise, I smiled to myself maybe this time Chris would truly be gone from their lives, Grand told my Mom that she would be here until the threat was extinguished But there was ache in the pit of my stomach somehow I knew this was far from over my mom went into her room to go the bathroom I followed her in there it was a macabre scene there where holes punched into the walls all over the room plaster was crumbling in several spots handcuffs, whips, and masks other items of torture I can't even name were all about the room some with stains of blood on them, I was shocked my hand started shaking I went into her room for the landline, My hand covered my mouth while I slowly backed out of the room into the corridor, What was all of that? I was confused had Chris done these bizarre things to my Mom, and had she willingly participated? I ran into the bathroom and dialed Aunt Julie's number and told her what I had seen, ok dear don't tell your Mom you called me I'm going to drive by and pick up Sophie and we will be there promptly! I said ok thank you, Aunt Julie! I don't trust Mom's judgment right now so much has happened, Aunt Julie said, the mystery has been solved now we know what he used to place fear in your Mother Oh My God! Kim, Grandma said loudly, where are you? I said, I'm in the bathroom Grand, I'll be right out. I whispered, I have to hang up Aunt Julie, she said pack a bag for each of you, okay honey I'll be there shortly bye. I said bye I looked in the mirror to compose myself flushed the toilet then opened the door I quickly packed, standing by my bed I glanced down tears welled up in my eyes, the whole scene was too much I finished in just the nick of time, Grand said, Kim what's taking you so long, I exited my room and ran smack dab into Grand she grabbed my hand and said slow down, I laid my head on her shoulders and said Oh, Grandma, how did

everything get this way? I asked her, my voice was small even to my own ears.

Chapter 9

Well that's a question I intend to find the answer to soon mind you soon. Grand replied, she turned and walked slowly back into the family room where Susan was whispering quietly to our Mother, Grand asked, are we interrupting anything? No. Mom, you aren't Mom quietly said. There was a knock on the door, Mom reluctantly walked over to the door and said, who is it? Your Sisters came the reply Mom flung the door open and she brightened up considerably they both rushed in talking at once, Grandma said, have a seat girls Kim go and get us all a cup of coffee I just made some fresh a few minutes ago. I took a tray out of the cabinet and got a plate, put some of Grand's delicious cookies on it and sat the cups on the table. My Aunts were talking, and they were brought up to par about the previous evening's fiasco involving Chris. In my mind protecting Susan was paramount I sat next to her, placing my hand in hers to reassure her she ran and grabbed the remote control and laid down on her stomach in front of the television Mom had upgraded a few months ago to a 60 inch HDT with surround sound it was so amazing and we loved it, the cartoon network Courage the cowardly Dog one of her favorites, laughing along with Susan for several hours allowed us to be just a couple of normal kids, But I knew in the back of my mind we weren't normal kids, we were far from it. I enjoyed the moment regardless of the mumbo jumbo, I started to relax. when my eyes opened I came to realization that I must have fallen asleep, I was in to the bed beside Susan, I heard her light snores smiling I snuggled deeper under the covers and drifted back off to sleep, Silently saying my prayers I thanked God for loving us and keeping us, Upon I could I could hear a ruckus in the other room, after an expedited breakfast, Grand and Mom informed us that we were being taken school shopping, Susan jumped up and down happily, I wasn't looking forward to it because I was attending a new school, the school board had a massive reorganizing I was one of the unlucky ones to be given the boot by my former school. Change was sometimes good, but I had a foreboding thought of this change and my instincts were always right, I grimaced at that thought. Upon arriving at the mall, I dove right in and commenced having a good time, what, girl didn't love to shop? We stopped in Forever 21, Dillard's, JCPenney, Old Navy, and too many more to name, Skinny Jeans were in, hoodies a must have, I received an array of crop tops from Aeropostale, Mom insisted that we get our hair done we went to Curvy Cuts, both of us grinning from ear to ear, Yes she had come with us but had stayed in the background not to bring unwanted attention to herself, Mom had finally caved in and had permitted me to receive the hairstyle I had wanted for over two years, We dined at Chili's for lunch which was "delish" after a brief break the shopping continued we bought Nike's, Chuck Taylor's to complete our "tennis shoes" we went to purchase boots were on the extensive list so you know we had to have several pairs of these and open toe sandals which I liked immensely, last stop was Wal-Mart last but not least I found the most awesome binder that came with stickers and a backpack that color coordinated with all my other supplies, Susan and I reminded Mom not to forget our locks for our lockers. She told me to pick her backpack with all the accessories and all items on her list I did exactly what Mom wanted, and she was delighted and so was I. By then it was dark, so we decided on Susan's favorite place it was "Mc Donald's" so we didn't have to go far there was one in the store I was glad because we were hungry! When we were seated, I let Susan talk and I answered at the appropriate times, every now and then I would glance up into Mom's eyes on the guise that we were enjoying her conversation but this one time we weren't, they looked shadowed and weary. But for our sake she put on a brave front, I will always thank her for that because Susan really needed it and I think she knew it. Grand and my Aunts walked up with their meals. They decided to join us on the last leg of our journey, everyone laughed and joked but I didn't, I knew Mom was faking but, to what end? Grand, sat right across from her and I was glad she would figure it out; she couldn't lie to her, No Matter how hard she tried. Mom said, Girls you have forgotten your "undies" we said, yes, we will go back for them, socks as well. Grand looked everyone in the eye and said, let's go and go they did Grand said get 15 underwear with bras to match! We said 15? She said, I didn't stutter. We went and got what she said but we had fun because we found the cutest bras and underwear possible, Wal-Mart even had cute socks. We got two packs a piece with six in each bag. But Grand was diligent in everything she did. She put on more bras and socks, we added more panties and gave her a thumb's up! We actually had about 18 of each, and for some unknown reason she had led us to get these nothing Grand did she did by design there was always a reason trust that she had done this time I just didn't know this time. We headed for the register Mom came in front and paid for everything not saying anything which was odd, But anyway we arrived at home late Mom said, Goodnight everyone and hurried into her room, we were barely I n the house so she must've known we didn't say anything Susan played along not even knowing she was on que, While we were away Aunt Julie and Aunt Sophie had been cleaning all day, no wonder they looked so worn out when they had joined us this evening. How did that happen? While Susan was busy going through her bags, by the way we had 12 bags each, I could've had less I would not have cared. But anyway I ran into the kitchen pouring me a glass of milk acting like I was thirsty listening intently as Aunt Julie was talking telling her sister and Grand that Chris had been calling all day and had even come by the house, they had called the police but he was gone when they arrived. Grandma was urgently saying, you need to come stay with one of us until this blazes over, that's when I realized that Mom had joined the group, her sisters said, I agree, Mom shoulders were shaking she cried silently, I quickly finished off the milk, I raced to the back and retrieved the bags I had stuffed into the closet. I gathered the toiletries and toothbrushes, waiting on a signal from the dining room. I sat on the bed impatiently waiting Engaging Susan in pleasant conversation in order not to alarm her. But that was only a matter of time before this huge ball of wax hit the fan. Whispering turned into a loud rumble when there was a knock at the door, everyone screamed, who is it? The male voice on the other side of the door said, its Aaron he was Chris's brother having met him on numerous occasions Mom said, what do you want? He said, I must speak with you! Chris is in dire straits motion detector lights had been installed so they looked out the blinds to make sure Chris's wasn't lurking about. So, Mom kept the burglar bars locked to Aaron with Aunt Julie and Aunt Sara adamantly standing by her side, Can I come in Angela? We are family after all! He was a tall brunette with crystal blue eyes, attractive yes, he was but that was as far as it went. He glanced at them with hooded eyes, his eyes held a serious sheen to them as he assessed them. Say, what you came to say I will not allow you into my home noticing as I eased my way to the door with it cracked so that I could hear, Susan had quieted her banter, She sat in the middle of the bed with her legs crossed stroking her bear "puddles". Aaron never once raised his voice, he spoke in a very confidante manner Ok Angela I completely understand he stated Since, Chris's has been asked to leave the first night he drunk himself into a stupor, the second night he took a bottle of sleeping pills in an effort to commit suicide, Aunt Sophie asked, Did he succeed? No, fortunately not! Mom said

Oh No! she ran from the door and slumped down into her chair, Look Aaron if it's sympathy that you want you will get none here! He has taken this family through a tremendous amount of suffering, He has beat my sister relentlessly unless you are here to tell he is dead we do not care! Aunt Julie said she glanced at him hard and said, we have nothing more to say, keep him away from my sister. Grand had stood quietly in the background and listened without interrupting suddenly stepping between her two daughters she said with a menacing stare at Aaron, "if he comes back here I am going to put something in his body he wasn't born with" IF YOU COME BACK THE SAME GOES FOR YOU TOO! Pulling her gun out pointing it at him, her finger on the trigger Aaron faced danger in the face and he stood a bit taller and said, I don't want to lose a brother! Page 96 Grand said, give up the ghost! You have lost him already; he is now manipulating you and doesn't even realize it. Chris said, you wouldn't listen! Aunt Sophie said, Tell Chris stop selling his crop because we aren't buying! Aaron shouted, He said some of his things are still here, Mom said, He's lying he took all his stuff. Do you suppose he is talking about my Visa I placed in his name well no, I closed that account and had his name removed from any and all documents pertaining to me? And he signed a prenup he will not be getting any more of a free ride here. Bravo Grand remarked now be on your way boy and relay that message that it is over. Aaron stepped off the porch and walked across the lawn to a blue Hyundai that was parked on the curve. I ran to Grand and Susan ran to Mom and we both said thank you so very much! I solemnly said, Mom it was only a matter of time before he killed you! All eyes descended on me, why do you say that Kim? I whispered to Grandma, her room you need to see it and then you will understand why I feel this way! Grand went to Susan and took her into the kitchen to distract her and had her help her bake cookies, meanwhile Aunt Julie and Aunt

Sophie went into my Mother's room Aunt Sophie said, Oh my God! Aunt Julie said what the f___? They examined the walls, the cuffs, the whip, and the blood spatters all over the room and on various tools to inflict pain. Aunt Julie said, always the warrior I'm going to kill him! I walked over to the door and shut it for Susan, Aunt Julie's eyes were wide with a reflection of total shock that was mirrored there.   They decided to take pictures and the Police were called again. Aunt Sophie stood in a corner, tears were bright in her eyes as she imagined the unspeakable horrors inflicted on my Mom. How could this have been going on right under our noses and we didn't have a clue. Memories flooded back. I had noticed the change in my Mom. It happened gradually, Chris should be given an Oscar he put on such a façade that he loved her. I TOTALLY AGREED HE WOULD BE BETTER OFF DEAD! In his current condition he was a walking shell of a man. Page 99 I hugged Aunt Sophie and guided her out of the room with Aunt Julie following closely behind. The phone started to ring given the circumstances no one wanted to answer fearing it was Chris. I ran over to answer the phone. I yanked it off the cradle and said Hello, with a slight edge to my voice when I heard Chris's voice. The hairs on the back of my neck stood straight up! Chris you're not to hold my family hostage any longer! He said, Kim you don't understand, I interrupted him and said Oh, I understand that you have been torturing my Mother, Mom and Grand gasped from across the room, Chris denied it, and asked, what you mean? I have no idea what you are talking about! When that didn't work, he tried to appeal to my intelligence.

Chapter 10

Obviously unaware that I had seen "the Rocky Horror Picture Show" Kim he screamed over me, let me speak with my wife! You can't keep her from me! Grandma grabbed the phone and hung up! I stood there for a moment in time and thought to myself, Honestly, I didn't really want to leave my home, but I understood the reasoning behind it. Aunt Sophie appointed me to bring the bags into the living room and I did as was requested of me. Grand said, you can stay a couple days with each of us and if you still don't wish to give up then, you can always sell your house! Mom Aunt Julie said, I think that is the farthest thing from her mind right now. Aunt Sophie said she may not have a choice! My Mother said, I know right. We all piled into Aunt Julie's car. She drove like we were in a presidential procession. Aunt Sophie was in the front and Grandma pulled up the rear, we were in the middle. I like the way they did that. The first night we went to the La Quinta Inn, our safety was paramount and with Chris coming unglued no one knew where he would land, land he would but it wouldn't be on us, Grand called the Police and let them know our plans, I think that gave Mom some sort of comfort, We settled in our room , they got a suite with three counting doors into one living area, it had more of a home vibe than a hotel, I was very grateful to Grandma, and my Aunts for that Our Mother didn't contradict any ideas that they deemed to be a safe course of action for us, Mom was dismayed at the lengths in which Chris would go, I may be young but I wasn't surprised at all, I had seen this coming long ago. Everyone abandoned their Facebook, Instagram, and twitter accounts. We were aware that he knew of our accounts with the world so wrapped up in social media, but not us! Will we be back home before school starts? We hope so Kim, no worries everything will work out for you girls God has not forsaken you! She replied. My Mother had taken a back seat

very seldom ever responding to our chatter, I adored my Mother, feeling helpless I

shrugged my shoulders thinking to myself we needed a sense of normalcy I was started to

understand that life wasn't always what you expected to be, Grand kept saying it was going

to get worse before it gets better and I believed it to be true. The phone rang loudly it was

Aunt Julie's husband Uncle Bob calling to inform that Chris had been by their house twice,

The last time he came to the door and asked for my Mother, Uncle Bob told him she wasn't

there and he didn't know where we were, Chris asked, If he knew where we were would he

tell him, Uncle wanted to present a friendly façade to Chris so he said, Yes I would tell you I

wouldn't want to keep a husband from his wife, Uncle said he gruffly tagged him on his

shoulder feeling a kindred spirit with Uncle Bob but loved us and he had though from the

beginning that Chris was wrong for Mom he said, he had felt it in his gut. He thought like his

wife they despised him, but as long as he was unaware of it, it might give them some insight

into what he was up to. Uncle Bob was on the speaker as he divulged what had occurred, I

glanced in my Mother's direction she was sitting with her head down, I noticed the more he

did the more he took it from my Mom. I felt it all so unfair, Granddad was silent for so long I

thought she was asleep, her eyes were on my Mom with an intensity. I sat back and studied

everyone in the room, Susan was asleep, Grandma suddenly suggested why don't we call it

a night? I don't know about the rest of you, But I'm exhausted, it's been a very long

horrendous last couple of days, and I must get some rest, I walked over and kissed my Mom

on the top of her head, she moved slightly her hand came up and brushed gently against my

arm, I joined Susan not realizing how tired I really was when my head hit the pillow I

instantly drifted off. My night was daunting it was inundated with disturbing dreams of

Chris chasing us every corner we turned we couldn't seem to get away from him, he was lying in wait for us, the dream was dark and luminous no matter how fast we ran he would be looming over us his breath rancid, he appeared unkempt, disheveled, I was gasping for air struggling to breathe Oh My! I crouched down low protecting Susan and My Mom as best as I could. Susan whimpered and mom was crying uncontrollably. Chris eyes turned a deep red, his teeth had a vampire look lengthening as we gazed on, I shoved them down this long corridor. I urgently whispered, don't stop for nothing! I heard Mom praying asking God, to have mercy on us. It rolled out for miles and miles with no end in sight. We ran like racehorses in the elite Kentucky Derby our legs having a mind of their own. Susan was in the middle of us mute and subdued, feeling her tension beside me, out of nowhere Chris suddenly popped up in front of us, we all started to scream as though one sound melded into another, My Aunt Sophie voice broke through but seem yet so far away, Kimberly wake up, Kim shaking my shoulders with all her might dark clouds were surrounding me as I floated to the top, Something or someone had a hold of my feet, I frantically tried to free my feet the more I tried it felt like I was emerged in quicksand, I was screaming inside but no one could hear me my hands were swiping at my ankles they were engrossed in the murky depths of sand, Kim wake up, in the background I could hear Chris laughing fanatically, taunting me, Grandma's voice gently said Pray ask God to help you, not a second to waste , crying out to Jesus, the darkness parted and my eyes suddenly opened reaching out for My Aunt Sophie, burying my face into her shoulders she comforted me gently, there, there, she said, I swallowed shaking my head back and forth silently thanking God for bringing me out of my reverie. We sat like that for some time, what were you dreaming about? She asked for a second and I briefly relieved my nightmare. She listened with a look of concern upon her face. I was very glad Grand or Mom hadn't heard me nor Susan she was still asleep, realized we were all worn out, quietly getting out of bed entering the bathroom, glancing back at Aunt Sophie before I shut the door I smiled at her so she wouldn't worry, I sat down on the toilet I wouldn't let this affect me this way, it seemed so real, so real in fact that I feel and smell Chris heated and rancid breath on my neck. Placing my face into hands, quickly flushing the toilet, turning the faucet on I washed my hands over and over again, Aunt Sophie tapped lightly at the door, asking Are you alright Kim? I'll be right out, I answered one thing I knew for certain is that I was not going back to sleep, I think she knew it also she said, let's go and see what we can find to snack on. There was a full kitchen so they had bought items to cook and lots of snacks. Yes a snack and I know exactly what I want. I exclaimed running from the room in all the commotion we had awakened Susan, she rubbed her eyes and sat up and not wanting to be left I turned and went back for her. I placed my hands around her shoulders talking earnestly to her. Soon Mom and Grand came to our melee, Aunt Julie last but not least helped to prepare various bowls of snacks and found a movie on the television that we all agreed on. I soon came to the conclusion that we only slept out of exhaustion; I filed that in my mind to ponder over later.Back to the movie it was a comedy, laughter was something we were short on lately, even Mom was laughing hysterically we were in dire need of it and we all took advantage of it. The mood was light and cheery. Susan and I ate our popcorn lying on our tummies in front of the T.V. Several hours later sleep would not be denied. I felt it pulling at me yawning and batting my eyes in order to ward it off. But it couldn't as I glanced over at Susan she was fast asleep again, my eyes slowly shut as I succumbed to it also, the room was quite a little too quite as I sauntered into the living area, Grandma was fast asleep on the couch I walked over and watched the rise and fall of her chest to ensure that she was fine just sleeping, I backed up on my tippy toes and Grand's eyes popped open and said Good morning Kim, what time is it? It's ten am Grand, Your Aunts left early this morning, Go check in on your Mother, drawing closer to the door I could hear my Mom's voice vaguely, I eased the door open she was in her bathroom the door was open, I overheard her saying, Chris I miss you too, she said, un huh, I will find a way for us to be together, I love you so very much Chris! I was shocked I stood rooted at the door. I ran out quickly and shut her door, my mind was racing so many thoughts were going through my mind, First and foremost Mom had been lying to us all, Somehow I had known she wouldn't walk away from Chris. Grandma was in her room brushing her teeth, she said Kim darling when the door is closed you must knock and wait for me to tell you to come in with a twinkle in her eyes. I said, I'm sorry about that but I have something to tell you, Grand said, what is it that couldn't wait? Grand continued to gargle her mouth out, she wiped her off she stepped toward me arching one of her eyebrows and said yes, I filled her in on what I had overheard between Mom and Chris. Grand said, oh No I was afraid of that! We must try to keep them apart much as I believe in being optimistic, but I believed Mom was too far gone, and I didn't know if we would ever get her back, linking her fingers with my own and pulling me to her side my thoughts were running amuck Mom and Chris were a combination that we couldn't allow just as Grand had said was up to us. After a hearty breakfast Mom joined us in some skinny jeans and a body fitting sleek blouse Mom had on a bit of make-up, she never has required much anyway we are glad you decided to dress for our trip to the zoo. Mom you look beautiful, Susan said Mom we are going to have so much fun! Her eyes were beaming, she was jumping up and down with excitement. Grand and I watched my Mom as her eyes darted her hands were fidgeting looking around for an avenue of escape! Mom said, I have to step out for a second. I have to go to the bank. Grand grabbed my Mom's hand and her keys in the wake and said, Angela, no worries we can stop in route. Mom was nervous as she thought of a way to get out of our clutches, but unbeknownst to her we were on to her and definitely not about to allow her to meet up with a fanatic again! Mom made a mad dash for the door we had already gone over in this scenario, so we were ready, she tried to no avail to convince us that she was feeling closed in. Grand said, that's why we are going out, we all needed some fresh air, Mom grudgingly decided to accompany us. Mom thought she had convinced us as soon as the door was opened Mom sprinted over to the car, taking out her keys, but not Fast Grand had removed her car key from the ring we were going in Grand's car. Screaming In anger when she realized they were missing, she asked Mom how you could. Grandma replied, you're going to thank me one day. Mom went into a loud rant about how we were trying to control her life and how she didn't want her to be happy by the time Mom had finally calmed down we had been sitting in the car for 15 minutes, We explained to Susan what we were doing and she understood and was glad for it. She climbed into the back her mouth was in a stern line with her arms crossed she pouted the entire time, she reminded me of a petulant two year old, Susan and I watched in awe because we had never in our entire life seen our Mom act like this!   we found her actions repulsive and annoying, Grandma showed us what true maturity was and for that I was ashamed of my Mom .Grandma turned the station to a very popular station 99.1 it played a variety of music lots of soft rock old and new, I smiled at Grand and she smiled at me in turn in the rearview mirror I had taken a seat in the back with Mom, Susan and I sang along with the radio after about 45 minutes we arrived at the Zoo. Grand parked and we got out.

Grand said, Girls we are staying together as a family not running off, we said, Yes Ma'am and she smiled at us she had bigger things on her mind. We saw a variety of animals, we took lots of pictures, we all had a good comrade spirit, all except Mom. She was quiet, and we knew she was mad but for once I didn't care it was very selfish of her to act this way. I was touched by the elephants how they nurse and care for their young. We especially enjoyed the meerkats. My all-time favorites are the Lions; they are such majestic beasts. We had lunch and continued to explore, I said, Susan let's tell them we are ready to go because I knew Grand was tired and I didn't want her to overdo it. We got tickets to come back for Zoo lights. That was a yearly celebration the Zoo had for the holidays. It was magical. When we arrived back at the room Grand and I had dinner prepared in no time at all Mom went into her room to call Chris when she came out, she was in a much better mood.   I decided to call my best friend, she was glad to hear from me and I her I told her about all my new clothes for school, Mom had bought me a pair of Mudd Boots I was so excited she told me her Mom had gotten her some too, we talked into the nights until Grand knocked at the door and said, Lights Out. I wondered to myself was she a drill sergeant when she was younger, smiling to myself of the thought of Grand in military dress, what I wouldn't give to see that, April asked snidely did you hear what I said? I said un huh. She said, no you didn't! What did I say? All I could come up with was umm she said, that's what I thought! Let's talk tomorrow, and I said ok goodnight! Mush brain she said goodnight pinky we laughed and hung up. The shadows from the tree branches outside my room normally would have scared me but I had prayed, and I knew God has us, so I got back on my phone and went on YouTube after charging up my phone. I laughed At the shenanigans that people did and posted hours later my eyes started to drop like they were being held up with toothpicks, I slept hard not even aware that Susan had, was in the kitchen at the table with Mom and Grand they were eating and laughing merrily when I walked in. Grand said Good Morning sleepyhead! Susan asked, what was I dreaming about you were smiling, I answered I don't remember! Sure you don't bumble bee I hadn't heard that in a while my pet name when I was very young, she hugged me and I hugged her back, Grand placed a big plate in front of me and said say your blessing, I ate with relish not once glancing up this is what families are made of not one for saying I love you often but when I do you know I meant it I said, I love you guys and they said I love you too, The door opened slowly it was my Aunts with my cousins Kelly and Kamwen, Everyone sat down with Kam and Kelly took their plates grand had made for them with my Aunts declining the adults went in the living area while we ate and caught up, Aunt Sophie wouldn't fathom dragging kids in the middle of the chaos we found ourselves in. family but that was ok I understood I had missed them Kam and I were one year apart and so were Susan and Kelly we were as close as cousins could be. The adults decided to go to our house we were glad it felt good to be back at home, I told my cousins about our new games they said their Mom was gonna buy them one also I'm like that is so cool, we went in my room and played games we had so much fun, Each of us won a game apiece we played until dinner Even though I enjoyed them I wanted to be in the other room so I could get the scoop on Mom. Aunt Sophie cooked dinner. We had steak and potatoes. It was good, most of the time my thoughts were on my Mom.   I didn't know how to help her to her tell it she didn't need our help, even I knew a man wasn't supposed to treat his wife that way, they wanted Mom and Grand to cook but to be honest all of them could cook very well my cousins helped their Mom cleaned the kitchen I offered but Grand said, take the night off and I did. We were discussing the drive-in movie and I said, I don't see what all the fuss is about, Aunt Sophie heard me and said girls used the bathroom and changed into clean clothes and were going on a mission and guess what it was, it was the Drive-In. It was awesome we went to see Black Panther it was crowded when you drive in you pay and Aunt Sophie picked a good spot not to close but not too far away either, there was a sound controller we hung it from our window we all went to get snacks what was a movie with Popcorn and other goodies by the time we made it back the movie was starting, I love Superheroes of any kind but he was special the movie was so colorful it was in a faraway African country where the technology would knock your socks off it was a great movie and we had a great time. Because we Had been on the move for days and days, I don't remember making it home and getting in the bed but when I came too I was indeed in my bed snug and warm and I felt safe and secure. I hadn't felt that way in a while. Grand had us all cleaning the house from to room except Mom's room I promised myself never to go in there again and what I had been wondering about is why after Chris had left why hadn't she restored her room, If I wanted to know it would be better if I didn't ask her she probably wouldn't tell me anyway, What's the point? We played our games until we got bored, so we hatched a plan to get out of the house, so we all went into the living room and kissed Grandma, she took it all in. There was no fooling her she said okay what do you want? Susan being the one with the softest heart she said Grandma, can we go to the park to play? and it was hard to deny her anything, Grand said, I don't girls, what do you guys think? She glanced around the room Aunt Julie said, I think it will be alright. Aunt Sophie said, Yes, they need to get out and run and play instead of being cooped up in here with us. Grand said, you can go, don't forget your phones! Susan said to Kelly they have installed a new jungle gym for older kids it's awesome, Grandma said, put on your tennis shoes instead of your sandals since they have a hard surface, and you will be running around, Girls be in before dark, we said we will, that's when it dawned on me that Mom hadn't said a word how odd. Grandma and I could speak without really speaking. I knew exactly what she was referring too. OK Grandma, we will be back soon. Susan and Kelly walked in front of us, even though we laughed and talked, my eyes moved constantly taken in our surroundings we ran all the way there collapsing into the grass laughing. because I had fallen down we got up and headed for the jungle gym. They loved the many tunnels and curves and angles that's what made it so much fun. It was built like a maze and the architect had designed and from my first time on it was a winner. Susan and Kelly ran over to the swings there was a small hill behind the swings, Kam and I went and sat on the hill from that particular spot we could see over the entire park, I liked it there because we could see anyone coming the park and anyone leaving it seemed to give me and advantage to see him if he was indeed following us, During our whole time I had a feeling someone was watching us. Susan voice rang for me to come and push her so of course I did I whispered to Kam, let's go push these babies she laughed softly and said Don't let them hear you say that we will never live it down, she closed her snapchat account and ran gaily up to push her sister's swing She screamed, I'm faster than you, obviously you've forgotten I'm eating my WHEATIES almost clearing the hill before she sprinted past me loudly gasping "I am best forget the rest" she said, she was so fast she leaned against the swing set while I got up off my backside and tried to appear unscathed there laughter billowed all around me, I touched Susan on her back and said, Whatever as I pushed her Kam joined me at my side and commenced to pushing her sister, rigorously as I did.

Chapter 11

Time seemed to get away from us, we had been so engrossed in having fun, I suddenly said, we need to get back. Can't we stay a while longer, Kelly asked I said, No, you heard Grandma! Kelly said, I'm going to call Mom and see what she has to say about that always wanting things her way, at the exact second an extreme chill go down my spine, Danger was in the air, it was tangible you could almost touch it, all the birds ceased to chirp there was a deafening silence that came across the landscape, I thought I saw a shadow in the tree lines up on the hill I took a step back to get a better look, Everyone glanced in the direction of the trees, Susan made a small whelp and ran and threw her arms around my waist, Kam said, What is it? With fear in her eyes! It's him, I said my voice had taken on a very harsh tone even to my own ears, my muscles tense Are you serious ? She quietly asked me, Yes, Girls grab your things, and let's go! One of you call Grand and stay together, we placed Susan and Kelly in the middle and we ran toward the entrance of the park like we had never ran before, Kelly and Susan started to cry, Kam said, piggy back them that way we can cover more ground we squatted down and the girls climbed on our backs, I said latch your fingers together around our necks and legs around our waist, I heard a motor revving up in the distance I knew that familiar sound, I snatched my cell phone out of my pocket as I ran and scrolled 911 and I realized there was a convenience store half a block away , the operator said, Police, Fire, or Ambulance I said, Police and briefly told her we needed them now, I told her where we were and what the condition of our situation was. After several long heart wrenching minutes, I could hear the police sirens, but we were not fast enough. We crossed the street, I glanced into the eyes of a madman, he screamed, in our direction Girls I just want to talk to you, give your Daddy a chance you know I would never hurt you. He said in a pleading tone, I Love Your Mother! He was getting close to us, his arms were flaying about trying to touch us, my heart started to pound in my chest, just when I thought all hope was lost. My phone led them right to us. I had never severed the connection, so they had heard everything that had been said. Fear had overtaken them, they were so scared, three police cars barreled down on us pulling alongside us. He had escaped again running around the corner the officers jumped and the one closest to me grabbed my arm, I felt my sister being removed from my back, and I sat on the ground while they assisted Kam with Kelly, I stood up my mind was in turmoil a female officer pulled in to her embrace she said, Are you alright, You are in shock and I fainted dead away, I woke up in the back of the ambulance, I could hear my Mom's voice as they whispered quietly. My eyes blinked several times, I moved my legs gently to alert them that I was waking up. Kimberly, are you awake my Mom inquired gently? Yes, Mom I croaked. My throat was so dry, the paramedic handed me a bottle of water, I said Thank you. Where is everyone? I asked between gulps of water. My Mom said, they're standing out here being interviewed by the officers. He got away. Mom stated, shaking her head back and forth. I am so sorry that you have to go through this I really am; she hugged me, and I hugged her back. The paramedics interrupted our reunion and asked Do you want to go to the hospital? He said okay but I must check your vital signs before I release you, He said my vital signs were normal, you must make an appointment to see your private physician as soon as possible Mom assured them that she would take me, the female officer came and sat in the back with us and asked me was I feeling any better, I said Yes, thank you Mom was busy signing the computer that I was refusing the ride to the hospital. The other Paramedic on my left I hadn't noticed him he had been here the entire time, I glanced at him he was blond with aqua colored eyes He was gorgeous in a another life he would have been perfect my thoughts strayed from him he removed my blood pressure cuff and assisted me and Mom out of the side of the ambulance where they were waiting to question me further, one of the made a comment that it was very unlikely that he will give up, I think it would be better if I take him back then this all will stop, we were all stunned at what she just said that included Aunt Julie, Sophie, and Grand. Officer Huff "the female officer" said Ma'am that's exactly what he wants you to do we would advise against it. Mom started to cry and tremble, everyone flanked her on both sides. I loved the show of solidarity and for all the support they've always shown each other. The K-9 unit showed up and several officers rushed off flashlights and guns in hand to continue to search for him, to be a part of something so chaotic was so surreal, it reminded of a crime show I had seen on T.V. The search was on for an hour or more but to our surprise he had evaded capture once again. My Mom hugged each of us but I got very little comfort from that I smiled at her and looked deep within her eyes what I saw was raw determination, Aunt Julie got Mom's attention Grand said, Kim and went to her side and relayed the tale of events, I could hear the worry in her voice I assured her I was fine Kam and her sister rode with us she sat in the front with my Mom and I sat in the back and held on to Susan and Kelly the chatter was almost non existence in the car we were to shaken up and tired everyone drifted off to sleep in the warmth of the car, But for some reason I didn't trust my Mom on edge I didn't trust my Mom, several times our eyes met in the rearview mirror she looked very forlorn grief struck me in the gut like a sledge hammer she drove into driveway totally shutting herself down Aunt Sophie and Aunt Julie came out to the car to help us by any means necessary, I saw the fatigue written all over Grandma's face and asked her was she alright? She gently smiled

and said Yes, I am. But there was no rebuttal about calling her Grandma that's when I knew

something was wrong. I felt it in her hug and her mannerisms something was off and for

the life of me I couldn't put my finger on it. The girls were shuffled off to bed, no one

mentioned dinner.   That's when a hunger pain hit me, I went into the kitchen and heated

up a fair amount of food Grandma came into the dining room and took her seat across from

and she just stared at me without saying a word. I moved closer to her and asked her are

you going to tell me what the matter is? I poured me a glass of milk, she answered, I don't

know what you mean. I said, yes you do. I don't want any small talk; I just want to know

what is wrong? I want you to be honest with me, she said, Don't I always? Yes, you do, but

there is something that you are keeping from me, so what gives? Well Kimberly, if you must

know at that very moment Mom, Aunt Sara and Aunt Julie came in from the back Mom sank

down in her chair she looked so lost, Aunt Julie put on a fresh pot of coffee, Aunt Sophie

poured all the adults except a cup, Grand said, there is something we must tell you, Grand

said. My instincts came alive knowing that whatever they were about to divulge would

change me for the rest of my life. I took a long death breathe preparing myself Aunt Sophie

said, Mother went to the doctor and he ran a series of tests and she had feeling fatigued and

lethargic with a dull pain in her chest on occasion, Well the tests came back today and the

several arteries leading in and out of her heart are blocked and she must have surgery. I

screamed Aunt Sophie and Grand consoled me. I hugged her not wanting to ever let go. She

is not stressed in any shape, form, or fashion Aunt Julie said. Do you understand? I shook

my head and head and dried my tears I must be strong for Grandma deep within myself I

tapped into the will of strength that I knew I possessed I pulled me hair back and put it in a pink scrunchie I commented, I am going to clean up the kitchen I told Grandma why don't she go and take your bath and rest, better yet take your bath in the morning rest now, She said, now who do you think you sound like, I said, I don't know and asked who do you think I sound like? Everyone said, Mother , including my Mom! She smiled and said if you girls need me Don't hesitate to wake me we said, We will but we knew we wouldn't she was too important to us, Grandma, had been under a lot of stress and it has taken its toll on her she smiled she got up and went in search of her room I was glad, the whole time we had been talking to and about Grand, Mom didn't even bother to join us she seemed to be almost in a trance she sat and rocked herself not much if anything to anyone, I knelt at her feet and said Mom every time I said her name my voice rose one octave higher, I decided to get close and personal I placed my hands over here's and said Mom I see there is a struggle going on inside you But it will get better, you will prevail, her eyes focused on me she lightly touched my chin and I said, I love you Mom and as Grand would say , The tide will turn in our favor. I've prayed about it I padded her hand Mom said, In the face of adversity you are indeed just like your Grandma, her strength shines through you, I know we haven't talked much lately, but I wanted you to know that I Love you we are all so very proud of you and I am so sorry that you had to endure such a frightening situation you were put in and in all sincerity I believed him Mom said with a smirk on her face Kimberly it's late go on off to bed school will be starting soon you must adapt to turning in early . I said, don't remind me! and then I tidied the area and said my goodnights and went into my room, Susan was sleeping with me normally I would've happy to retreat to my little sanctuary, But the earlier encounter with Chris had unnerved me sitting on the edge of the bed I removed my shoes and went in and brush my teeth and got into my pajamas I crawled in with my sister she snuggled deeper into the covers snoring lightly I welcomed it tonight, I rolled onto my side and thanked God I had survived it all and that he would give me the strength to be able to deal with whatever was on the horizon. I woke to the beautiful sound of my Grandmother singing. I jumped out of bed with a jubilance I hadn't felt for quite a while. Breakfast was served and eaten within a short amount of time. We rushed to bathe and dress for church. We sat and waited patiently for Grand and Aunt Sophie Aunt Julie had gone home early this morning. So when they came in Grand greeted us with a smile she had on a teal dress, with matching accessories Aunt Sophie had on a blue dress with the same they both looked beautiful, But Grand quick as always to compliment us said, Girls you are so pretty! My feet felt awkward

But, I wanted you to know that I love you and we are all very proud of you, and I am so very sorry you had to endure the frightening situation that you were put in, Mom said, in all sincerity I believed her. Kimberly it's late go on off to bed school will be starting soon you must adapt to turning in early, Mom said with a smirk on her face frowning I said, please don't remind me! Reluctantly I made a beeline for my room, normally I would have been happy to retreat to my little sanctuary, the earlier encounter with Chris had unnerved me, sitting on the edge of bed I removed my shoes and went into my bathroom and brushed my teeth and put on my pajamas, I crawled into the bed with my sister she snuggled deeper into the covers snoring lightly, I welcomed it tonight I rolled on my side and I thank God I had survived it and I asked God to give me strength to deal with whatever was on the horizon I finally drifted off to sleep. I woke to the beautiful sound of my Grandmother singing, I jumped out of bed with a jubilance, I hadn't felt for quite a while. Breakfast was served and ate at no time at all, Mom and Aunt Sophie rushed us we bathed and dressed in

Sunday's dresses and we were sitting waiting patiently when Grand came in the living room, She said with a huge smile on her face, You girls look so pretty, my feet felt awkward, but it was no sense it bringing it up, we were going to church and there was no way out of it I thought I would try so I said, I don't feel well. Grandma said, really she came over and placed her hand on my forehead and commented, You do not have a fever, Kim I'm so sorry you're not feeling well, But the good news is we are going to church and we will pray for you and by the time it is over, you will feel much better. Laughter burst forth from my family, I smiled and joined in with the rest of them, Sunday school was my favorite, after it was over there was an intermission, Then the afternoon service began the pastor had chosen to talk about the prodigal son it was a very good but after a while my mind began to wander about life and what the school year would bring on one hand I was excited on the other I was apprehensive, as Grand would say sometimes it's not the place that's bad but the people in it. My sister tapped me on the shoulder, the collection plate was being passed around, I went in my purse and retrieved the money, Mom had given us money to pay the offering and the tithes I always loved to make sure I gave my share Because God had been so good to us. Since I was young, I remember Grand discussing the importance of giving and how God would bless you, I willingly gave and believed. We all stood for dismissal prayer, my cousin Kam said, I'm glad that is over! Aunt Sophie leaned over and said, I heard you, watch your mouth. She hung her head without comment and managed to look ashamed, I linked arms with her and casually strolled out of the church at the entrance the Pastor and his wife where greeting parishioners he always had a way of making you feel you mattered he hugged each of us and said, I haven't seen you guys lately glancing at us, Grandma said, yes we are to rectify that we all knew what that meant the adults went off with the Pastor and the first lady and the choir director encouraged us to come to choir rehearsals we promised that we would, Several girls we hadn't seen since school motioned us over and we went and chatted it up with them after several attempts to get me to talk I decided why not and I was glad I did the conversation was fun I actually was shocked Nicole and I were never friends she was one of the mean girl's best friend to my nemesis ,Carmen said hi Kimberly she was nice. Yes, she was! But in my heart of hearts I knew it was a ploy but play along I did. No matter what games her and her crew had planned for this year they would soon find out I wasn't an easy target. Brandy interrupted us again and she asked many questions revealing very little about herself we soon caught on and ended the conversation and went in search of our extended family, finding them in the car.

Chapter 12

Mom asked in an anxious tone, where were you? Susan ran to her and gave her a big hug and she said we were with some of our friends catching up. Relief was written all over her face Aunt Sophie was in the car talking quietly to Grand, Girls let's get a move on. We laughed and talked all the way home, We undressed and put on shorts and tanks and got on the Xbox and played for a couple of hours, I was very heavy hearted Because I knew after dinner they would be leaving Grandma went to her room for some rest, Grand was absent I was very worried about her so I knocked and went into her room she was in the bed sound asleep . Closing the door quietly as possible hoping I hadn't disturbed her. I went into the kitchen and assisted Mom and Aunt Sophie in preparing dinner We were having. Chicken, braised potatoes ,grilled greens with almonds and rolls I made a cheesecake this morning for dessert, so I set the table and calledeveryone in for Sunday dinner. Grand was already up, she said, I will be out in a minute. We arrived at the table at the same time. I stood back and watched my family, everyone was relaxed and cheerful and that in itself made me happy. After dinner Aunt Sophie said, Kimberly you are singing, I haven't heard you sing for a long time, she hugged me tightly and said, Wow! I sang a song we knew and loved, Celine's Dion song from the Titanic. I sang with all my heart the notes were so pure you could almost see them in midair as the last tune filtered forth, I was glad for the reprieve from all the chaos, Girls you can relax because we aren't leaving today! Kelly said, Mom what about school? Kam said, I'm glad! Aunt Sophie said, no worries, I will go and get your clothes and school supplies for school tomorrow! I knew. deep down that Mom was putting on a façade for us, more days were slipping by she was becoming more and more withdrawn, I glanced up into Grand's eyes and she was a very shrewd woman she was taking it all in so I smiled at her she smiled back, that's when I realized I was the one to have to take Grandma's place she had been grooming me for it I had been taught by the best I would step into her shoes I may never be as formidable as her but I would be diligent and I would strive to make her proud, I had noticed that Grand had ate quite a bit I was happy that her appetite had returned, Grand and Mom and Aunt Sophie had retreated to the living room while us kids cleaned the kitchen put the leftovers away with no fussing and gripping now that was a shocker! I was nervous but I had prepared everything for tomorrow. I ran in and sat next to Grand. I had popped a bowl of kettle corn. It was delicious Mom had ordered the western channel for Grand she was elated she was watching the one and only "John Wayne in StageCoach," we enjoyed it. This was our moment, we were the only ones in there, everyone was busy with their own individual tasks, I loved her, and I could not imagine my life without her. At nine Mom told us we had to take our baths and get in the bed. We kissed and hugged our Moms but Grandma we gave a special hug and kiss she laughed and said, enough already! Off to bed with you and stop stalling, she motioned for me and whispered Kimberly we will talk soon I whispered back and Ok, goodnight. I followed Susan in the room our cousins were examining their clothes trying to decide what to wear for the first day of school. I had decided on a pair of pink skinny jeans and a frilly top. My backpack was also pink and pink sandals to complete my ensemble. I had four new pairs of shoes, two pairs of tennis shoes, and four pairs of boots that's not include my massive amount of clothes. I would say I had enough to start the new school year off. I had gotten make-up this year but I didn't wear a lot just some Kim Kardashian's mascara and some mac lip-gloss I had purchased several colors Grand had always told me that I was a natural beauty, I don't know about that, but then again Grand was never wrong I smirked to myself, it made my heart sing to see Susan so happy, we all took turns taking our baths, There was a knock at the door it was Grandma she prayed with all of us we were settled in our beds we welcomed it because we knew she felt much better, after the prayer she asked, What we were smiling about, we said, Oh, nothing Grand! We snickered, she said Enough good night chickadees! We said, goodnight Grandma! Mom and Aunt Sophie stuck their heads in the door and said, goodnight as well. We quieted down after that we were all tired, we whispered until we drifted off without worrying and pondering over bad things. It was a goodnight's rest. The morning came without delay we all arose in good spirits racing to brush our teeth and wash our faces everyone fighting for the bathroom before we finished Mom called us in to eat, Grand was at the stove cooking breakfast Pancakes and sausage, Oh boy my mouth was watering the banana nut pancakes were the best they were indeed my favorite. We ate as fast as we could, we kissed Grand and my cousins hugged us and followed their Mom out of their car. I applied my lip-gloss and grabbed my backpack I changed my mind and pulled on socks and my Chuck Taylor's they were converse, I knew my best friend would love them I shrugged my shoulders , I gasped and I hugged Susan she glanced at me said, she told me not to worry she would be ok! I made her promise that if anything happened, I said anything, no matter how small she was to call me she gave me a thumbs up and said, ok worry wart, you sound so much like Grand you know that right? She asked, I replied, I consider that a compliment with a big smile on my face. Mom and Grand were in the car waiting for us looking annoyed, I smiled and climbed into the back , I asked, you both going to drop us off, Grand turned in her seat and asked, do you have a problem with that? I answered No ma'am she smiled, Mom didn't drive as fast as Grand she took her time and drove, we hated it , today was not a day for complaints. We arrived at Susan's school, she jumped out and ran over to her friends, she was very popular at her school, Mom went into Susan's school to get her schedule, there was a line going into the parking lot of Westside High I said my goodbyes. Mom said, Kimberly hurry up you don't want to be tardy on the first day of school I said ok Mom, she asked if I was nervous, I hesitated and said, a little bit. Westside was a very big school sported brown bricks on the left side of the school it a huge grassy area where lots of the student body where gathered in groups talking amongst themselves and hanging out I placed my backpack on my shoulder I glanced around the school was in a prosperous part of town so a lot of students were zoned to this area this made for a large school population, Westside was known for having some of the best teachers and school was known for graduating their senior class to go on to Stanford, and a lot of the other Ivy league schools so I was going to take advantage of being at the best and learn much as I could to have a very good future for myself put my phone in my front pocket there were so many new faces I walked over to the right side of the flag pole and I heard my name being called. Kimberly, she said, I glanced in the direction of where the voice came from. It belonged to my one and only true friend April, she ran up to me and we hugged each other. A tall blond guy by the name of Kurt said, you guys are so dramatic! We glanced at him and said, I know right! He looked sullen and said, whatever and walked away we laughed and talked non stop until the bell rang, A thought crossed my mind about what I had been going through at home with my Mom, I wanted to open up about it, But today was not that day. We headed for the gym. The principal was giving a speech and so on, He told us several changes were made this year one was if you were caught on your phone during class hours your phone would be confiscated and you had to pay ten dollars to get it back. No one was exempt, everyone had to comply. If you threatened another student, you would be expelled for three days if it happened you would be expelled for the entire school year. If anyone was involved in a fight the police were called and you were taken to jail. If you were caught skipping school, you were expelled for three days. The groans could be heard all over the gym, Stealing last but not least if you are caught with another student's things for the entire school year, phones and computers were commonly stolen and sold to other students if you were caught buying stolen items the same punishment applied, One of the guys whispered loudly, I guess I better stop stealing. The Principal asked, who said that? No one said a word!   The tutor program had been expanded and the tutors were paid 10.00 an hour, Mr. Douglas said, I thought that would be, and incentive for more of the student tutors to sign up to help others. Everyone started to clap, I thought it was a great program because not all students came from well to do backgrounds. All the classes were split into groups from the freshmen class we were all being given our homeroom teacher and our schedule, by the time they called us juniors I was bored and anxious for it to be done with I was in line next to April we chatted it up until I was next in line the teacher said next I was overjoyed I was given Mr. Schwab for Science and Algebra, Mr. Ryan for Math, Mrs. Barnes for History, Mr. Bencroft for Health and Reading 11 Mrs. Russell for Music Mrs. Michaels for Culinary Arts for my elective I had picked Journalism I was given all the classes with my choice teachers so it couldn't get any better than this and I would sign up for tutoring sessions so my day would be full April and I were ecstatic all our classes were together our morning quickly flew by, April Kim I'm famished what about you? I said, Ok the cafeteria here we come, ours was one of dreams in front of the cafeteria was a massive wolf we were home of the wolves! The school served a meal but you were given several choices, there was a pizza hub, the culinary class had their own restaurant of sorts, and there was a small Fuddruckers each month the restaurants changed, we both decided on pizza she a cheese and me a pepperoni I was a carnivore so meat it must be. We both grabbed bottled water, I loved the one with alkaline in it. We were not drinking carbonated drinks too often. We ate catching up but just when I thought it was safe to go back into the water a cliché the sharks started to circle Nicole and Carmen walked up with Nicole saying, Hello my favorite Lesbians! I said, you wish! You act like one more than me. I often see you with your girlfriends. I stared each of them up and down and said, Menage a trio, is that how you swing? Everyone started to laugh. Carmen said, you are going to pay for that, I said No doubt! and took a bite of my pizza in a nonchalant way. April leaned over and whispered, don't anger them! I kicked her foot under the table because Nicole was looming over us with a very vicious look on her face, Nicole stood over my shoulder and said, the games have just begun! I said you guys are attention seekers and self-absorbed, Nicole said in a loud whisper Fuck you Bitch! I flicked my hand in the air like I was brushing lint off my clothes. Carmen called them and they followed her like obedient puppies, the cafeteria exploded in laughter. This is going to be a very interesting year I said, my voice dripping with sarcasm. Kim got a move on we mustn't be tardy on our first day she was always one for protocol. I slowly walked to our <u>lockers,</u> turning around suddenly I asked, are you angry with me? She said , no but please don't antagonize them, don't let them make you mad!   Shrugging my shoulders, I chose not to say anything, we had been assigned our lockers earlier, I was glad we were on same side and we closed our lockers and went quickly Mrs. Bundy was us

The gym teacher and the girl's cheerleader coach and basketball coach had her plate full. April said with a small smile I hope she is a good juggler! April played softball and she ran track she was good, Tosha had been put into our class she had been transferred from Worthing at the end of last year, true enough she didn't like me but I think she was feeling a little lost in a new school so this year I had decided to reach out to her, I knew what it was like to feel alone and isolated and left out like the whole world was moving fast and you was standing still, Tosha I said, Tosha I said her name again she pointed to her wireless earbuds she paused what she was listening to and said in a very small voice, Yes, April went and sat next to her and asked, How was your summer? She smirked and said Why do you care; you guys are nosy! She brightened up considerably and said, we went to Montana! She said my Aunt lives there and she has a horse ranch, Wow April said, that sounds like fun! She asked April did she ride? And April said yes, I've been riding since I was very young. I said Do tell. We all laughed, it felt good to see her smile. We laughed and talked Mrs. Green had to split us up. she informed April and I that she had moved from Montana and her first school in the state of Texas had been Worthing High the curriculum was much better here and she was glad to be at Westside she told me there were a group of girls that were mean to her we smiled because we were sure of who they were. I told each of them I was staying after school to talk to Mrs. Green, April stayed with me but Tosha could not because her Mom was coming to pick her up. The next class was our homeroom normally I would of taken a front row seat but not this year I went to the back row, April sat in front of me and Tosha sat across from me soon as we were seated Carmen, Brandy and Nicole walked into the class they saw us and they walked up to us, Carmen said, you in our seats, I said I don't see your names on them, Nicole glared me like she wanted to slap me but I was standing my ground, Brandy said you obviously don't realize who you are messing with a wide smirk on her face and bumped into my desk. The teacher came in and said students take your seats, they reluctantly sat down they found three seats in the middle of the classroom, they whispered and glared at the us I shook my head and focused all my attention on the teacher, everything she said was very relevant and I'm glad I listened at the end of the class she assigned lockers to the students that still didn't have one while we whispered quietly to each other, at this point I wanted to talk to April alone concerning Tosha. The final bell rang for today and we all filed out simultaneously. I felt extremely happy it had been a very uneventful day, other than the run in we had with Nicole and her cohorts. When we arrived at our lockers we exchanged numbers OURS Moms were waiting for us and we would not keep them waiting needlessly we said goodbye and linked hands and ran for the entrance April was very touchy feely and sometimes I was embarrassed about it but I hadn't seen her in a while and today was the first day at school so I refused to dampen the mood. I saw Grand and my Mom almost immediately they picked Susan up first that lifted my spirits even higher I waved at April and jumped into the back seat, Susan was talking earnestly I glanced at Grand paying close attention to her appearance she looked healthier before she looked a tad peeked due to her heart but I could tell she was feeling better I smiled then I listened wholeheartedly as Susan gave us a rundown on her day she was happy with all her classes except one. Her homeroom teacher was Mrs. Harris I remember her, she was a small woman with a larger than life personality she was her English teacher also. Mom interrupted us asking if we would like to stop to get a bite to eat, we said yes and Susan asked if we could go to Dairy Queen, I agreed thinking I could taste my burger already we had always loved it But Mom had stopped our frequent trips there because of Chris.

Chapter 13

My eyes misted over but I couldn't let him steal my peace of mind I thought on how he had changed our lives I felt sorrow but I turned that channel in my brain, blinking rapidly I glanced up into Grand's eyes in the rearview mirror her eyes narrowed, I believed she knew what I was thinking matter of fact I knew she did. I smiled at her, there was no one like Grand and I was glad there wasn't. after arriving there we ordered and ran to the ladies room to check my appearance making sure I was up to standards I often saw students from my school I don't know why it was so important to me now it never mattered before I guess I was growing up it would be nice if I had a boyfriend no I was not ready for sex, I was waiting for the right person to come into my life but to have someone to talk to share things with would be nice, there were boys that had shown an interest in me but they were the wrong ones and I had let it be known they weren't the one even the more persistent ones gave up over time. Being the ice queen wasn't something I was proud of the age old fairy tale of falling in love with a white picket fence and a couple children to make my life complete that thought had a certain ring to it and I liked it, so much for mulling over things because my burger awaits and smell of it was awakening my senses I ran out to join my family they were still standing at the counter Susan was placing her order I had already ordered a DQ burger with the min they brought out Mom's new order Grand said, I'm going to put Dairy Queen on Facebook because their food is so incredibly good she told the cashier that, the young man said Ma'am don't do that but he looked like he wish that she would I laughed so robustly that everyone smiled with me Grand said, you are so young at heart and that's what we love about you and I said, I know right!   Toward the end of our meal Mom's phone rang and she looked at the screen and said Wow! And excuse me and she stepped away from the table Grandma suddenly became very quiet but I kept talking to Susan not wanting to alarm her but I knew it was Chris, nothing really touched Mom to the point it made her jump for joy nothing except Chris that ass-wipe and a few other choice words that I could think of as Grand would say and she added after saying that a real lady never uses vulgar language I smiled at that very thought because I knew she would come mighty close to that invisible line if not leaping over it. Grand asked Kimberly what's on your mind? I said, I was thinking about an old saying someone had once told me, she said, Oh really! Somehow it always came back to her, smiling to myself, we ate the remainder of our meal in silence each of us, I'm more than sure were, all thinking about my Mom. She rushed back into the restaurant without actually looking us in the eye. Grand ignored her and asked Susan what sport she was going to try out for this year? She said Cheerleading and Softball, I replied you're a girl my heart smiling at her she I knew you would be happy because I'm following in your footsteps I glanced at her and said I want you to follow your own path and do what you like to do Susan I am this is something I have always wanted to do, I watched you and I just fell in love with Cheerleading and gymnastics, I looked in her eyes intently, and said I know right I'm so proud of you! And whatever you decide to do I will support you to the fullest! She leaned over and hugged me and I said with a smirk and a sharper tone there will be no more of that! Grand had been listening to our banter. She said I am glad you realize that family is everything and you must always help each other. We both glanced at each other and said, yes ma'am that one word ruffled her feathers she responded I am not a ma'am! We all burst with laughter, Susan and I jumped up and ran to the counter to order sundaes because I knew Grand wanted to a few minutes of alone time with my Mom we got our ice cream cones and took a seat across the room from them they talked for a while with Mom make gestures trying to win Grand over to her way of thinking but it wasn't working we finally ran out to the car and went over her schedule with me I knew she wouldn't be disappointed with her classes I was overjoyed for her. After some time, Grand and Mom emerged from the restaurant Mom had a look upon her face that alerted me that it hadn't gone well for her, Grand probably let her have it. We rode home in silence But Grand not one for being melancholy got the conversation going with some exciting news she would be moving in expediently and under no terms would she move out she said she was in it for the long haul we screamed she said if I had known I was going to receive this kind of reaction I would have moved in long ago we grinned I hugged her she said watch out sit back down and fasten your seatbelts. Susan and I grinned shamelessly. Grand pulled into the driveway and Mom and Susan got out and went into the house I took my time and stayed with Grand so that I could talk with her I said if you need me at any time I will be here she replied I couldn't ask for a better granddaughter I love all my grandchildren but you hold a special place in my heart we are so much alike if I've said it a thousand times I've never meant it more I just don't want your Mom and her decisions to affect you in any way I shook my head and said Grandma I said don't want you to take on more than you can handle she said I will not she grabbed my arm I noticed how slow Grand was moving my little sister was indeed growing up.

I heard her encouraging Grand to sleep in one of the guest room she had declined saying in a snarky voice that she wanted to be out in the open the real reason hadn't escaped me Susan had already made up the couch because that's what I had intended to do but I eventually had my way we walked in and I took her purse and without any fuss she went into her room and prepared herself for bed we did the same thing we had our baths before I went in mine's I reminded to Susan to get her clothes ready for tomorrow, she smiled and said Ok not giving me any sass, Kim, Susan said, I will be glad when I get in high school because I hate wearing a uniform I know you dislike it but don't be in a hurry to grow up I said, Because the older you become the more issues you are faced with ok I said and hugged her she frowned but she hugged me and turned in for the night. I came out of the bathroom fresh and a tad bit tired but I had a small project to do in one of my classes I got it done I must check on Grand I thought to myself, I knocked on her door she said come in, I walked in and sat on the floor beside her bed she leaned over and said Kimberly I am fine just tired she lifted her hand and lightly touched my head I laid my head on her arm and said Grand I love you with all my heart she smiled and said ditto we both giggled like school chums I sometimes wish we were sisters we were so alike I couldn't imagine my life without her! not that I didn't thank God for Susan I did Grand was more of a Mom to me than my own Mom But since I was checking I had better check on Mom too I didn't want her to feel left out, I knocked on her door after a minute with no answer I peeked into her room Mom was fast asleep I ran in and kissed her on her forehead and I took a quick look she had cleaned up all of that graphic material and it looked like her room a sigh of relief escaped me before I knew it I whispered I love you Mom and snuck back out of her room shutting the door quietly. I walked down the hallway humming and smiling and then climbing into my bed Susan was already asleep. I said my prayers asking God to heal Grand and to bless our home I prayed for everyone all over the world. I don't remember going to sleep but my dreams were dark and turbulent and it seemed to be no end to it there was no one in my dreams but I could hear that same maniacal laughter that always sent chills up and down my spine I tossed and turned all night woke to Susan saying, Kimberly wake up, my eyes felt like they were glued shut managed to pry them apart I headed to the bathroom I placed eye drops in my eyes after washing my face I gazed in mirror at my reflection, I knew it was going to be one of those day flashes of last night kept entering my mind I said aloud, No! I wouldn't allow my dreams to dampen my day. I closed my mind off to it, there was a room with a red door in the back of my mind. I saw myself opening the door just a "smiggen" of a crack mind you that's where I stored the bad things that I went through and had seen in my life and this is one of things in which I had to store these thoughts mind you this room was not a refuge but it prevented my mind from breaking down and I felt it kept me safe it may seem illogical but it worked for me that's what mattered most. I heard Mom outside of my door, girls' breakfast is ready! Grand was at the stove making waffles and sausage. She had a bowl on the table filled with strawberries she made a special glaze to accompany the waffles and to top it off scrambled eggs with cheese. Good morning Grand and Mom I said, they both replied in turn good morning, I said Grand you out did yourself Wow! She said I believe I did! I set the table and poured everyone some milk, I asked even you Grand she said, yes even me milk makes you healthy and strong and as the commercial says with a smirk it makes your body feel good. Time is of the essence I placed platters on the table and Mom said the blessing and Grand said, dig in! she didn't have to tell me twice we ate as fast and humanly as possible. Susan and I ran and dressed for school. After dressing I applied my lip-gloss and mascara. I chose not to overindulge in makeup, always using a bare minimum of products to look as natural as possible was my mantra. I grabbed my backpack and placed my hoodie inside some of the rooms were rather chilly, Girls it is time to go mom insisted, I said Yes ma'am and we giggled we heard grumbling on the other side of the door opening the door Grand said, I'm not a ma'am! With a stern look upon her face but there was a twinkle in her eye I knew it was a lot of bark but no bite! Susan grabbed Grand around her waist and glanced up in her face and said Grand you're a mess! She replied I know right! We have to get you guys to school! I kissed Grand on her cheek and we ran out to the car being late for school was not an option. We arrived at West Briar Susan leaned over and gave Grand and Mom a quick kiss and said her goodbyes to us Mom was usually engaged on her phone her head was bent she was reading and sending texts, Susan glanced sadly at Mom and then she jumped out we watched her go into the school, I was wondering who she was talking to But I knew in my heart of hearts it was Chris but deep down inside I knew he was not going to give up, I had more important things to think about I looked down at my skinny jeans they complimented me to no end, I was excited at how the jeans fit me I'm not mundane or basic I'm a girly girl, I loved dressing up and looking pretty. Grand said, you have a nice day Kimberly and I looked at her and said bye you guys smiling I climbed out of the car I was shocked the line in front of the school was almost diminished I knew the bell was about to ring I ran with the speed of a track star I didn't stop at my locker I ran into my class and took my seat just as the bell rang April and Tosha were smiling at me, the morning rushed by all my teachers gave me homework we headed for the cafeteria we went to the culinary restaurant we ordered the spaghetti, green beans, salad and garlic bread we sat down April said the spaghetti smells delish I picked my fork and said it smells as good as it tastes! Tosha asked us about our weekend activities? April regaled us with several funny tidbits. I decided not to be so forthcoming so I talked about the Dairy Queen trip and they laughed and we finished and went to our lockers we were talking when an extremely handsome guy came up behind Tosha and said Tosha she asked, what is it Simon? He asked, do you have any extra pens and pencils? She said sure you need to keep up with your things better your always losing something reprimanding him, April and I were awestruck we started without actually trying to stare Tosha said Simon I want to introduce you to my friends Kimberly and April he smiled at us he smiled a 100 watt smile at us he was blond with hazel eyes with longest eyelashes I had ever seen on a boy in my life he glanced at April no interest there for him but when he glanced at me up and down his eyes went focusing on my breasts I am very busty but his attention was embarrassing to me so I stepped back I started to blush I said Tosha we are going to class we will catch up with you later she said ok, let me talk to this louse with a huge grin on her face we didn't have next period with her so that gave us time to talk April dragged me to the nearest bathroom and I collapsed in her arms Kimberly he was gorgeous! I said Yes, I think that was my husband and we both laughed, April said no he isn't he is shallow and self-centered I picked that up on him right away. his aura was dark, he's not the one for you, I said Ok! Ok! I hear you April she said gesturing wildly with her hands hear me well I am serious she finally said after shaking her head for several minutes I said I'm over it we have to get to class before were tardy and on the second day April said my Mom will let me have it I checked my hair more and more girls started to file into the bathroom we had less than five minutes before the bell rang so we had no time to spare we ran out moving like we had fire on our tails the teacher was calling the class to order when we walked in Mr. Schwab our science teacher young ladies take your seats unless you wish to stand for the entire 45 minutes we sat in the last row next to the windows, He said for all of you students that are new to my class in case you didn't know this will be most exciting class you be having all day, Several of the students smirked all that knew him were used to his shenanigans he was indeed a very colorful fellow he handed each of us a schedule and the subject manner we would be covering April looked at hers and said Oh my! She was in heaven this was her favorite subject. Mr. Schwab got up and went to the board and explained to us about the meaning of science and what it meant to the world as a whole. I'm ready to get into the thick of things. My mind started to wander. It was a beautiful day. And outside the rays from the sun were glinting off of the blades of grass on the school lawn something darted past the corner of the building turning my head in that direction that's when I saw Chris he was standing in the shadows fear struck me to my very core I grabbed my phone to take a picture of him when I glanced back he was gone blinking rapidly I realized he had been there spying on me that in itself gave me the willies I scanned the entire side of the school almost like he had vanished into thin air I went to the window and place my hand on the window pane I was so lost in thought that I had forgotten my surroundings I heard Nicole say in the background I told she was a basket case where did he go? I thought to myself but the roar of the class brought me back to reality Kimberly can you come up to the board and figure out this science equation for me, Mr. Schwab asked me and I got up and I was reading it before I got to the board I picked up a piece of chalk and wrote my answer and Mr. Schwab said thank you Kimberly and the example is if you do not pay attention in class you will be at the board working until the end of the school year do you understand me I said yes, and next time Kimberly you might want to let us in on absent mindedness I said I was looking at the sun wishing I was down at Jamaica Beach lying in the sun working on my tan Everyone had something to say about that I caught April's eye and from her look I knew she knew something was wrong.

Chapter 14

Mr. Schwab said summer is about over, and school is in session. How about that? We all laughed he had a way of differentiate any situation and that's why I liked him so much, taking my mind off of the obvious I watched Mr. Schwab walk to the head of each row and he handed out a paper for each of us which they passed back , it covered a lot of what he had went over today instead of bringing up the fact that this was our second day we all closed our books no comments could be heard he was a teacher totally about his students learning and we all knew it. He said when you finish place it on my desk and I will see you guys tomorrow read Pages 1-5 in chapter 1 there will be a quiz class dismissed April grabbed my arm and we headed without haste to the door as we stepped out into the corridor I shook my head in an effort to banish the shadows from my mind Tosha walked up and got in the middle and linked arms with each of us and we all laughed and I think at moment I needed it. The next class was my study hall I went into that class with and agenda and that was to help others normally it takes several days for them to compile a list of students that were in need of help I glanced through the list I choose two candidates ones that were teachable and wanted to learn there were only a small amount of students that had signed up to tutor I had hoped that more would jump on the band wagon because the need was far greater than some knew or cared about but I was very eager, Samuel Evans was from a single parent family home I knew his Mom worked very hard to give her five children a better life I wanted to help him, some of the students made jests about him and his sisters because by today's standards they didn't always wear the latest styles but they were all smart and that's what made them unique they stuck up for each other I admired that if you fought one you fought them all and that was great, Because sometimes the older ones forget the younger ones but not in their case, they all looked for the others I admired that. I went back to my seat. April had been watching me. She asked Kimberly what is wrong? I told her nothing! She decided not to pressure me. We both took out our books and I tackled some of the vast amount of homework in which we had. Time went by at a steady pace and we were soon dismissed for the day. We all met at our lockers and we chatted for a minute then we bid Tosha goodbye. April and I walked to the front. She hugged me today was a good day she said, kimmee I will call you later I said ok I waved goodbye. Not wanting to keep Grand and Mom waiting too long I sprinted off the sunshine beckoned to me, Someone stopped me at the entrance not wanting to ignore her but in the back of my mind I tried to pull her up in my memory banks and pull her up I did, she was Nicole's sister I smiled politely and listened for a minute before she lost my interest a person that talked very fast without actually saying anything I said I have got to go she said Oh Ok I smiled and felt a wave of relief at our brief encounter immediately stepping out from the shelter of the doorway I felt a chill go up my spine and end in the roots of my hair, feeling alarmed as I glanced around in dismay that's when I spotted him at the corner of the building he was wearing a black hoodie and it was almost covering his face but I saw his eyes staring at me I stood still gathering myself then I inhaled and I darted off in the direction of My Mom's car I jumped into backseat without delay Grand asked, Kimberly is everything alright? I shook my head reluctantly and said Yes, I grabbed Susan hand and held on she felt me shaking she squeezed my hand back and I glanced at her she could tell that something was wrong, really they all could Grand drove out of the parking lot with caution But I realized that her mind was on me I would not worry her I struck up a conversation with her I said, Guess what I am going to tutor this year, she said that's wonderful dear smiling but it didn't quite reach her eyes I talked on and in depth about several things concerning the new school year, Susan finally interrupted me she proceeded to tell us about her day. I suddenly realized that my Mom had not said one single thing to me, but I wouldn't let her mood swings or lack thereof affect me. Grand engaged us both with conversation and her wisdom she made us feel as though we mattered I loved her for her intuitive especially for Susan's sake Grand asked if we wanted to get something to eat we declined, all becoming very quiet engrossed in our own thoughts, Several dark thoughts descended on me, would we always be reminded of my Mother's blunder oh sure we all made mistakes I wasn't totally blaming her but in the back of my mind I knew she was the one blame for the chaotic state of affairs we had found ourselves in even if an abuser refuses to leave you alone, somewhere sometime you must come to the conclusion that they will never change, no matter that she tried to make light of the situation we knew that this was serious and if Mom refused to come to terms with our dilemma then I must. Because it was up to me to protect my little sister, she didn't ask for this more and more everyday he gave me numerous clues that this wasn't over, and truth be told it may end very badly for us. It felt like we were shrouded with a dark luminous cloud hanging over us Kimberly, Kimberly Grand was calling my name with aspiration in her voice I glanced up wearily and made eye contact I shook my head slightly she understood me more than anyone did, she didn't protest she just let me enjoy the protection and the closeness of only being with my family could bring, I closed my eyes for a second but when I glanced at her again I saw a light of recognition there and I was glad she left it alone for now, Susan as usual filled us in on one of her many tales I eagerly listened because she needed someone to acknowledge her, Mom was glancing out of the far window like she was unaware of any of us. Grand and I were knew she was struggling to make a decision to take Chris back, love must be a beast it seemed to hurt you and all that you hold dear I wanted no part of it at least no time soon anyway, I wouldn't go as far as to say never because even to my own ears that would be unrealistic. We felt the car accelerate it suddenly lurched to the left and Grand whispered, Oh no you don't, Kim and Susan you girls lay down in the seat and close your eyes we ducked down without question we heard the alarm in her voice, I peered over the seat and gazed into the eyes of a madman he was veering over into our lane Grand punched the gas we passed a black Honda we started to weave in and out of traffic my heart was thumping hard in my chest. Grand placed several cars between us and didn't I tell you it is Chris, Mom suddenly came out of her reverie and asked What's wrong Mom? Why are you driving so recklessly? Grand said, oh you noticed! Did you? Mom glanced in the backseat at us and asked What's wrong with you girls, why are you laying down in the seat? Finally taking in her surroundings she glanced out the back window of our car just as Chris drove up alongside us, Mom's eyes mirrored saucers making her face appear peaked, Chris screamed, old woman pull over I want to talk to my wife, you can't keep us apart, Mom gazed at Grand and said I need to talk to him Mom, Mom continued to ask the same question numerous times I could see the strain on Grand's face, I sat up and said Grandma pull over and let her go please! If you ask me, I said she was already gone. Susan had finally sat up. She was holding on to me. She was crying softly. Anger exploded all throughout my entire body, I said when you go Mom don't come back, we don't need you! Grand pulled over, Mom never uttered a word as she got out of the car, without looking back, Susan said Mom please don't go! Grand pulled over at the and said you are a sorry excuse for a daughter I was holding that back forever get out she screeched at my Mom Chris hollered

"woman are you coming are not"? Susan huddled up against me and I held on to her. She

leaned out of the window and said We love you Mom! Mom shrugged her shoulders and

opened the door to Chris's car and got in with him. He was nervously glancing around

because he knew the police were looking for him, Mom glanced at us briefly he smiled but

it was a smile of malice and they drove off. Grand apologized to us she said she was sorry, I

said Grand it's ok I understand she is your daughter and you are disappointed Grand said I

will not allow her to drag you guys down with her, Susan said I love her and I will pray for

her I said I will too Susan she looked at me then glanced out the window for once she

wasn't her normal animated self and that made me sad. That's when I noticed the tears

streaming silently down Grand's face, we both leaned over the seat and hugged her. She

tightly hugged us back the silence was deafening so thick you could cut it with a knife we

then went home. We both took our time getting out of the car we walked slowly with Grand

she opened the door and we went in I put my backpack in my room and said, I am going to

prepare dinner Grand please she went into the living room and sat on the couch I was

relieved because I knew Grand and Susan had been through a lot so I turned on the

television but I put it on mute, I then turned on the stereo Grand loved classic rock it was

her favorite so Aerosmith was playing and I went and started dinner and I started to sing

softly I had to take their mind off of that fiasco that they had witnessed. my voice rose and

octave with my sister's voice joining in and last but not least Grand's alto rounded out our

trio while I washed the chicken I already had put peeled several potatoes on for my fluffy

mashed sour cream potatoes and I put them in a pot we sang like our lives depended on it

we soon had smiles on our faces laughing joyously I went over and set the alarm and also I changed the code and wrote down the new one and I gave Grand a copy of it. Now we were

the only ones who knew it and Mom would not be able to come in and because of her

mindset now that thought made me happy, Susan came to the table with her books and

started on her homework I smiled to myself Grand came in and grabbed a frying pan from

the overhead island rack and put in a significant amount of Olive Oil and turned the burner

on she placed the , chicken into a bowl seasoned it up and rolled it around in flour, I then

cut up some fresh organic green beans and put them on, it will take too long to prepare

fresh rolls but I have some in the freezer put them in the oven for 15 minutes when dinner

is almost done I told Grand ok, just when I thought it wouldn't get any better the radio

belted out "You got that loving feeling" Grand said OH Yeah! Now we jamming! she started

to jiggle her hips a little I smiled and kissed her on her cheek Grand said she bumped into

Susan with her hips she glanced at her and Grand said it was a dance in my day called " the

bump" Susan jumped up and we all started to dance she said. Oh Grand you made that up

laughing Grand said, No I didn't in my day everyone did it, the dance was simple and fun I

glanced at Susan and Grand, she finally was sitting down after a few bumps I danced and

put on such a display until they stopped in complete shock I decided to give Grand a

reprieve she smiled and said, you girls are too much I got up turned the chicken and

finished the rest of the meal in no time flat I put in the rolls and Susan set the table and

Grand poured juice and milk with dinner in front of us I solemnly said the blessing I made

sure to ask God to take care of Mom and keep her safe in Jesus mighty name I said the

prayer because I wanted God to repair the damage that had been done to our family we

lifted our heads our eyes were shining with unspent tears but that was ok too smiling I ran

to stove and retrieved the rolls I had almost forgotten them we all felt much better and I thanked God for that we ate and talked gaily we started swapping old family stories that brought happiness and left smiles upon our faces we stayed at the table for more than an hour Grand was tired so I sent her off to take her bath while Susan and I put up the leftovers and cleaned the kitchen with a diligence I hadn't felt in a while I felt a renewal in my spirit we all could use a lift sometimes I made sure the burglar bars on the windows were latched and the shutters on the windows were closed.after this I went into my room and finished my homework while Susan had her bath I then prepared my clothes for tomorrow when she came out she slipped into bed I said goodnight I knew she would be asleep when I came out of the bathroom I took a lengthy bath I dried my hair and a walked to my bed and got on my knees and talked to God and thanked him for all the blessings he had bestowed on us I wanted him to know how much I loved him I then got in the bed and turned over to the wall that's when I allowed my tears to flow freely asking God to strengthen me and help me make it through this, I knew he would I was exhausted to my very bones much as I hated to admit it I was scared for my Mom it's was as though someone had taken over my Mom's body and this person was a stranger to me it pains me to think these thoughts I must try to take on as much as I can because I knew Grand wasn't able to do it try as she might I knew Grand would not give up without a fight, after a few minutes I finally went to sleep. Breakfast was quick. I ran and brushed my teeth and washed my face and I dressed in extreme care. I chose my orange leggings with a matching shirt and a khaki vest Susan said Kimberly you look adorable I said thanks sis! I grabbed my backpack and purse Grand was at the front door waiting on us, Susan ran past me I yelled for her to wait in truth I didn't want her to go outside without me hearing the command in my voice she stopped dead in her tracks she turned I saw the fear written all over her face, But Grand always one to diffuse a situation said, Girls come here and she placed her hands in both of ours and she continued I want you girls to have a great day at school, Do you know how much I love you both? And I will miss you but you need not worry about your old Grand, I'm going to go home and check on things there and I will be back in time enough to pick you up from school pulling us to her. She kissed us and gave us a big squeeze and said, Now let's go! She got us dropped off. I thanked her and made her not to do too much today and she assured me she wouldn't think of it. I smiled and she asked Who me? I answered Yes you! I jumped out and made it to my first period in the nick of time Kimberly thank you for gracing us with your appearance the entire class laughed But I knew it was in good humor the teacher gave us a worksheet and book assignment I loved this because I didn't have to listen to a lecture instead not only would we get more accomplished it also made the class go by much faster I finished my work glancing over at April her head was still immersed in her textbook I smiled and glanced at the other students when suddenly the teacher asked Kimberly, are you daydreaming? I slowly shook my head no and went back to my book almost laughing. He said Kimberly please enlighten us on what is so incredibly funny? Is it perhaps that F that is on the horizon? I said aloud with conviction No Sir! He studied me for a moment and said well, then let's get some work done! You have only 15 minutes to finish and the time starts now, I raced through my reading and my pop quiz simultaneously glancing up at the clock, Then I glanced at my teacher this teacher was old school with no phone as a backup we placed our phones on the desktop facedown, smiling I worked diligently attacking the easier problems first and hardest ones last finishing up in 14 minutes flat placing my pencil upon the desk April and I finished. We were masters and that's how we had always handled tasks. Each row passed their quizzes to the front the teacher took them in hand and asked the class How many had read the assignment and had managed to take the pop quiz? Without any fanfare about six of us raised our hands he said, I see Honest I like that! The bell rang and I believed we were all glad as we filed out of the class stopping off at my locker Tosha was there waiting with her brother , as much as he got under my skin I decided to play it cool and ignore him she approached us and we chatted amicably her brother rudely interrupted us and loudly said my name, Kimberly he said again I answered Yes, he smiled at me I felt a hotness engulf my entire being and I went up in flames. Tosha said, Brothers! Can't live with them but I would rather live without them she smiled glancing up into his eyes please pay no attention to him Kimberly Tosha said, there is a new one every week don't fall for the hype! He conquers them and discards them all in a week. She smiled at me and said I don't want you to be a victim to him ok and linked her arms with mine April and I glanced back at him as I walked away. Tosha, I said I want to thank you, she said no problem with a huge smile at this point in my life I needed nothing to distract me. We parted ways and we both said Goodbye walking into my next class. I sat down immediately. April opened her book, but I was sort of in a daze. It went by without any hitches. The next class was gym.

Chapter 15

 We changed and came up upstairs and Mrs. Bundy told us to set on the mats it was tumbling and walking the high beam we tumbled for a while then she told us to take a minute and we talked amongst ourselves walking up she sat in the middle of us and she said Girls cheerleading tryouts are in two weeks now who wants to tryout I raised my hand also a there was a lot of other hands I was excited April I said, tryout this year she said no I will not this is not for me I said ok, Mrs. Bundy said ok girls lets practice putting several of us into cheering groups, and she put others into groups that did practicing on the parallel bars then she walked us through some cheers, it was so much fun we laughed and encouraged each other. the coach said you know I am cheerleading and basketball coach we all looked expectantly at her she said it will be an new experience for some of you but others I will say to you welcome back we smiled and April and I gave each other a pat on the fore arm laughing she ok class dismissed went to the lockers and changed class ended exited the gym I said that was something we will remember for the rest of our lives she said what gives why did you ask me to you know I wouldn't I said I want you to step out of your zone I glanced at Nicole she was watching me with a vague look upon her face I glanced away I shrugged my face! I am not in the mood, April said they are so extra! Page 231 I said I have so many other things on my mind the events of the day smiled at her deserve much better but anyway, she said I been thinking about what you said and I said ok tell me I want you to apologize to me rather than argue with her I said I'm sorry it was daunting that didn't want to tryout but honestly I understood her reasoning behind her decision, my friends went on the last class for the day, I made a mad stop at the restroom being so caught up in everything I hadn't been all day and it felt as though my bladder it going to burst I went into an empty stall and I placed tissue on the seat and I made haste and sat down as urine flowed freely from my body I got up and wiped myself clean I heard April calling me she said Kimberly, Kimberly I asked What? I'm in here! You're wanted in the office, I said ok I came out of the stall washed my hands and checked my appearance and said I'm on my way I ran out of the restroom I was told to stop running by the hall monitor so I stopped walking briskly to the office I rounded the corner and through the blinds the blinds I saw my Mother she was very pale opening the door I stepped into the room, the tension was so thick in the air I could've cut it with a knife something was wrong I could feel it Mrs. Palmers the school clerk said, Kimberly your Mom is here to sign you out early I sternly glanced at my Mom but I decided to bring it down a notch I slide a false smile in its place and said ok Mom. I placed my hand in the small of her back and led her out into the corridor. She walked over to a seat and we sat and faced each other. I asked What's wrong Mom? She said your Grandma was rushed to the hospital a couple of hours ago she is in the emergency room at Hermann Memorial I wanted to pick you up first so that we could talk privately, Chris is out in the car and we are going to get Susan then we are going to go the hospital I sucked in a ragged breath and asked, Are you serious right now? She whispered Yes, calm down with anger in my voice I said, it doesn't matter to me how you decide to live your life, but he is a dangerous Mom and you know it, I jumped up and said, You're not my Mom! Her face flushed, she hung her head and said please don't say that, I love you! I said you don't love me, you only care about yourself! I lunged at her she cowed as if I had struck her I witnessed fear in her eyes I dropped down in front of her and said if you care about me at least think of Susan I said harshly You're so fucking selfish all you care about is him screw the rest of us I clamp my hands so tight I could feel my fingernails penetrating my

skin I close my eyes and said, it doesn't matter even as I muttered those meaningful words I

knew it wasn't true. Mom got up and arranged her clothes never quite never making eye

contact she said one thing you said wasn't true I love each and every one of you I backed up

and crossed my arms and followed her sullenly out of the front entrance I saw his car as

soon as we walked into the parking lot He was frowning at my Mom her feet suddenly took

flight like the hounds of hell were upon her and to think about it that's exactly what he

resembled I glanced into his eyes and they radiated menace I could see the impatience in

him his fingers tapping the wheel as we approached he asked, What took you so long? You

know better than to keep me waiting! Pausing for a moment she cleared her throat and she

stepped aside so he could see me Smiling in my direction if you want to call that sneer a

smile My Mom visibly trembled and in his wake he said Hurry up and get in I have to pick

up my other daughter he said with an intensity as he looked at me in the eye that made me

feel way too uncomfortable, I slide into the back seat his car was so clean it was almost

pristine I had always heard that the cleanliness of your car reflected the personality of its

owner then this was a severe contradiction to the word I thought to myself we rode in

silence to West Briar I went inside with my mom to retrieve my little sister my Mom and I

stood in line there were several parents ahead of us, I whispered to Mom asking her if she

cared for herself and if so Why was she back with that ass-wipe? My Mom face turned in a

motionless steel mask, But I was undeterred by my Mom actions because I knew deep in

my heart I had no desire to see my Mom hurt, but somehow someway I had to get through

to her and make her come to terms about the terrible decision she was making Susan came

into the office with a dismayed look upon her face when she saw Mom, her jaw dropped and she jumped and ran over to her and hugged her tightly I said Sis she glanced up at me and asked, So what's going on? Mom said come on after signing the papers she said, this conversation is for your ears alone, several people silently stared at us I opened and walked out while my Mom and Susan followed me out of the office Mom turned to Susan and blurted out your grandma is in the hospital! Chris and I had to pick you girls up to take you to the hospital to see about your Grand, Mom shook her heads slightly and started to play with her purse straps a sign that showed she was truly nervous, Susan slipped her hand into mine's something she always did when she was overwhelmed, I held her hand in mine and pulled it up a little to let her know I had her! We walked out to the car. If she was surprised by Chris' presence, she never let on we climbed into the backseat Mom said, please take us to the hospital! He said, Not right now woman I'm hungry! Mom angrily said, ok let's have fast food and drive thru because we must get there asap! Watch your tone! He said sharply! He turned around and asked, Ok girls, where do you want to go? I answered for both of us and said, we don't care! He didn't even acknowledge me he was staring at Susan; I was worried there was something on his mind and I knew it wasn't good! How I wish Grand was here oh no! Grand I was so mad at Mom I hadn't thought of her! I thought sadly, Grand please be ok! We love and need you desperately! Susan pulled her hair behind her ears and stared off in space he angrily took off revving the motor like he was almost mad, every fast food restaurant we scoured had all their parking lots brimming with cars, I said What about What a burger? They had a few cars and it wouldn't be a long wait, Chris told us to get what we wanted. Food wasn't on any of our minds we ordered for fear he would get angry. I monitored him closely giving attention to the fact when we came to the window to pay he put the palm of his hand out and my Mom placed twenty five in his hand he gave the pretty cashier a smirk and a wink obviously this was something that my Mom was accustomed to because she didn't get upset trying her best not to notice the cashier passed four bags out the window along with our drinks Susan and I had ordered a milkshake with a water Grand had always reminded to keep hydrated with plenty of water, the cashier said Sir your change is $4.92 he leaned over and said Darling you can keep the change, Mom said, Chris we may need it! At this point she had been nonchalant about his behavior the cashier adjusted her headset I could sense he was starting to make her feel uncomfortable she said bye Chris drove off with a frown written all over his face we drove thru rush hour traffic we got on the beltway we were in line to pay the 1.25 he said I didn't know they raised the prices Mom paid and he received a receipt he threw the paper into the air we had been riding for over ten minutes I nagged Susan she watched me pull a book out of my backpack staring on my homework she followed suit we were both speed readers and we loved learning Suddenly Chris glanced over his shoulder and said Baby girl I was going to help you with your homework she glanced up and said No thank you! Kimberly is the brain in our family if I need any help, she will help me! I tousled her hair and she gleefully laughed. He met my eyes in the rearview mirror. What I saw mirrored there was malice pure and simple he frightened me, but I would never let him see it. Susan leaned into me and asked me a question about a math problem. I glanced over her worksheet,I told her to do the easy ones that she could do herself to start on and the harder ones I would help her with and she actually did that. Susan was always in a hurry to finish. That's why she sometimes had problems understanding a problem. She was smart. I knew if she slowed down she would do better in math. I explained the problem in the simplest of matters she soon caught on and finished it in no time flat. I glanced up and I told her to grab her backpack we pulled into the Hermann Memorial parking garage Mom turned to us as we placed our books into our backpacks Girls we can't stay long your Grandma is going to need her rest Susan said ok Mom can we go now? I didn't even bother answering her I rolled my eyes instead we got out of the car and waited at the rear bumper for our Mom I glanced into the rear window because it was taking Mom so long to join us I saw Chris and Mom both face to face they were extremely upset I Mom got out of the car I grabbed Susan's hand and walked in front of our Mom we got on the elevator and arrived in the front lobby and we went down a corridor to another set of elevators Grand was on the fourth floor, we walked into Grand's room I expected to see her all plugged up to all sorts of machines but I was happy Grand was sitting up in bed smiling Susan stopped in the middle of the doorway her hands covering her mouth while tears flowed down her face. Grand held out her arms and we gladly ran into them. She hugged and kissed us. That's when I noticed my Aunts, we spoke to them and Mom said to her Mother Wow you made a speedy recovery! But something about the way she said that nagged at me for many days to come. But Grand only grinned and said That's right! And I'm waiting on my discharge papers and that means you and Chris are no longer needed, Mom looked aghast and I'm going back to house with my grandbabies looking fondly at us, But Mom she stuttered and asked Who will take care of you? Why do I have two other daughters we will manage! Grand said snidely Mom turned to her sisters and asked How have you been? They said fine, Thanks for asking and started to laugh! Mom looked embarrassed. Aunt Sophia said, you can go, no need to worry we will make sure they are properly settled in. My Mom turned and looked at each of us and said Well I never! Then stomped out of the room in a haughty manner. Grand said, Child you never will! We all laughed. I suddenly turned to Grand and asked,

Were you really sick? Glancing in My Aunts direction she asked Can you go get me a cup of coffee? my little sister jumped at the chance to do something for Grand she followed them out Grand took a deep breath and said that was a diversion, I shrugged she continued your Mom and Chris came to the house this morning right after you left for school they said they came to plead their case with me even though my instincts told me not to let them in. I did anyway and they came in we talked all of 15 minutes and your Mom asked for a cup of coffee now you know that was right up my alley, I made a fresh pot and I poured each of us a cup suddenly your Mom said she wanted to talk to me privately and I took her into my bedroom not wanting to leave Chris but I did! She sounded so sincere she was so compelling she told me how she wasn't happy with Chris and that he had deceived her on so many occasions and how she wanted to come back home, Grand said I was so happy I couldn't believe she was saying these things so we hatched a plan and went back into the kitchen and we sat at the table each of us sipping our coffee when out of nowhere I felt very warm I started to sweat my heart start to palpate your Mom asked me if I was alright? I remember I said Yes, I stood up and a wave of dizziness overcame me. It was like I was having an outer body experience where I could see what was happening to me, but I couldn't do a thing about it. Everything seemed to move in slow motion when I woke up I was alone I was so weak I dragged myself to knees and crawled over to my phone I called Sophia and she called Julie and the ambulance was called when I came to again I was in the emergency room the doctors did a series of blood tests then they got the results back they came and told me I had been drugged and I could have died, Chris put something into my coffee the doctor said it was enough to knock out a mule. I feel a little woozy but other than that I am as right as rain I was shocked my body started to tremble, she grabbed me and said I am alright Do you hear Me? I shook my head up and down and they gave me something to counteract the drug. I will be fine! I hope she wasn't saying that to spare my feelings they walked back into the room and Grand had a huge grin on her face we all engulfed her in a group hug! Susan asked What did I miss? We all said simultaneously Nothing! She said Sure I didn't we all laughed we took our seat on the bed next to Grand they chatted while I thought about what Grand had divulged to me I was shook to the core I was horrified that my Mom was willing to poison her own Mom for a man I was disgusted with her and I knew I couldn't have anything else to do with her but for now I wanted to enjoy Grand and for her to know that we loved her. We started to get a little restless the nurse walked in with my Grand's discharge papers she said to make sure that my Grand doesn't overdo it we said we would, Grand took her time getting off of the bed I could tell she wasn't quite herself But we would take care of her and make sure she made a quick recovery Aunt Julie went to retrieve the car from the garage we waited in the front lobby for her she sat down and we talked and she pulled up and ran inside to assist us with Grand, Grand said, girls I can walk much as I thank you I only need one of you to lean on and she choose me I smiled at her she winked at me I know now without a shadow of a doubt in my mind that Mom wasn't to be trusted never would I make that mistake again she was so enthralled with Chris and no matter how hard we had tried it had been to no avail but for the life of me I didn't fathom the thought of giving up on her but that was my secret I thought to myself as we drove home. Needlessly the wheels in my brain refused to stop turning I must come up with a plan I was still thinking by the time we pulled up in Grand's driveway Aunt Sophie's car already there Aunt Julie had informed us that she was moving in and I was glad we must be diligent because Grand needed us we must combine our efforts and take care of her until her strength returns we were told to go our room and get our things ready for school tomorrow while Aunt Julie prepared dinner I wasn't really hungry but I would eat something so they wouldn't be worried about me, We called in to eat Grand was sitting on the couch with a tray in front of her I was just glad she was here. We ate and talked she had cooked fried chicken and it was so good I walked over and asked Grand if she needed anything else she assured me that she didn't I smiled and took her tray she said goodnight and got up and went to her room if anyone was surprised they hid it well Susan and I cleaned the kitchen then went to get our baths no realizing how sleepy I was until I finally got under the cover I said my prayers thanking God for loving us and keeping us safe my thoughts once again went to my Mom, I somehow had to get my Mom away from him by any means necessary because if someone you know and love wanders off into the darkness even though you may be afraid of the dark sometimes one must venture off into the black void to retrieve the one that had lost their way to return them to the light my mind was in a quandary leaning back against my headboard I went back into the kitchen and made me a warm glass of milk Grand had told me long time ago what to do to rectify this situation I drank it and wiped my mouth and I went into Grand's room she was asleep so I went off to join her in la land smiling to myself I climbed into my bed noticing that Susan's eyes were closed so I plugged in my phone and placed the earbuds in to hear some inspirational music I listened until I arrived in la la land. To my dismay I slept very little when I finally did wake up it felt as though my eyes were glued together from the lack of sleep.

Chapter 16

   She pulled herself up and sat on the side of the bed holding her head in her hands there was a knock on the door she said come in and Grand stepped into the room and shut the door Susan was already up so we were alone I glanced at her and all the chaos and fear and the need to keep all those you hold dear safe it had finally taken a toll my body started to shake I ran to her and buried my face in her shoulders cried tears started to stream down my face it was like a heavy rain after a long drought she led me to the bed and she held me in her arms and said now, now, it's going to be alright I cried sorrowful tears she consoled me softly with God's help there is nothing that we can't do without him she said we will prevail Chris will not destroy this family and took me by my shoulders and stared at me looking deep in my eyes and said you must believe and remember that I said yes ma'am and she smiled at me I hugged her and jumped up and went into the bathroom I heard the door quietly close and she left my room when I came out of the bathroom I was dressed Susan was in the room she glanced in my direction I asked what was wrong she said she had heard me crying I noticed that there were tears glistening in her eyes I swallowed and said to her please forgive me I felt weak she said one you're not is weak what you are Kimberly is human and that is what we do when we are sad and overwhelmed. I glanced at her intently and asked what have you done with my little sister? We both laughed gaily we went into the kitchen Grand had made us breakfast sandwiches and fruit we ate quickly and went and washed our hands I grabbed my backpack and we headed for the door Aunt Julie met us at the door she said good morning sleepy heads I'm going to take you to school Grand told us to have a good day I was concerned about Grand being alone but I knew she wouldn't open the door if Mom and Chris showed up again she stood at the door there was love written all over her face but I glimpsed steel beneath that gaze and I was very happy for her allowing me to see it at this time of peril we all needed each other's strength we would gladly give it to turn the tide in our lives Aunt Julie wasn't saying much and I understood why she reminded us to call her if we needed her I had heard her say she was going home for the day to check up on things and Aunt Sophia would pick us up from school I certainly was glad for their help but I knew my Mom was taking us all through a lot but enough of that I said goodbye to Susan I jumped out and ran into the school I ran to my locker there was no one around the halls were deserted I knew I had a couple of minutes before the bell rang I ran into my Home Economics class in the nick of time I was glad because it always seem to lighten my mood even if I had to share the class with some undesirables glancing quickly at Carmen and Nicole and their entourage my mind was always on high alert but that was not the case this day or I would've noticed Nicole's foot I tripped over it. and I started to fall I tried to right myself but I only made it worse I grabbed a hold of an empty desk but instead of using it for leverage I pulled it down on top me and laughter erupted across the classroom April ran over to help me up and I allowed this because it would have been unkind not to she said Kimberly are you alright? I said Yes I am when I took my seat I could feel eyes boring into me but I choose to ignore it Mrs. Russell gave us each a pattern book and we had already bought our cloth we worked on sewing our aprons mine's was pink and April had a chosen a multicolored cloth but it was pretty we whispered and worked until the bell rang Nicole walked over to me I braced myself I wouldn't let her see the hurt and embarrassment she had caused me and said you're very clumsy I answered only when bitches are involved she smirked with a hard look in her eyes

I glanced at her with venom in mine knowing one day I was going to have to fight her, I

didn't wish to but I knew they wouldn't leave me alone and that in itself made me antsy

April grabbed my arm as we exited the classroom she said thoughtfully why is it when they

are messing with you the teacher never seems to see them I shrugged my shoulders and

said I haven't the foggiest we laughed going in search of our next class we stopped off in the

girls restroom we walked and used it quickly while we were washing our hands. Carmen

walked with Nicole glancing at us. She said to me you are so basic I arched one of my

eyebrows and asked you are what again? I saw a flash of anger cross her face not getting

the kind of response she was hoping for April whispered to me she is so mean I hate her I

said hate is such a strong word no, worries let me handle it turning in their direction I

smiled at them with a harshness clearly shown on my face and said in case you didn't know

let me bring you up to speed I am the wrong person to fuck with Carmen's eyes narrowed

and she said Any day anytime bitch I said you call it and I will be there we stood staring at

each other until April said Kimberly we better get going and I answered let's do that April

said after we were in the hallway they are getting worse and I am worried I said I'm not she

knew me and what I was saying was true she nervously fiddled with her books I glanced

around us knowing this had gone far beyond a game and every game had an ending

thinking defiantly to myself we went to gym Nicole ran up and bumped into me hard Mrs.

Bundy witnessed it all she said Nicole you and Kimberly come here April went on

downstairs to dress for class walking quickly over she said I will have no more of this rough

housing from you Nicole and anymore I will send you to the principal office but for today

you have detention go take a seat and not another word out of you she was a small statue of

a woman but when she spoke no one defied her she walked over to the bleachers without another word she knew Mrs. Bundy was not the one she sent me to hurry and change.

asking me beforehand if I was ok I said yes I smiled at least somebody had noticed what

they were doing to me I was tired of I but anyway I joined the rest of the class we had fun

even though I noticed Carmen on more than one occasion staring at me I had often

wondered to myself what had I done to make her dislike me so I wouldn't entertain bullshit

because I knew I had done nothing wrong to her realizing that when someone does that

there is something fractured within themselves maybe she was being abused at home I

wish I could help her but I knew she accept no help from me sounding like a skeptic even to

myself I would pray for her I revealed my thoughts to April she said that she knew

something was off about her sometimes that's the only thing you can do but I was always a

firm believer in keeping your friends close but keep your enemies closer I couldn't afford to

bury my head in the sand about this matter but I wouldn't let them ruin my day. We did

gymnastics I glanced at Mrs. Bundy I liked and admired her a lot we teamed up in pairs the

period slowly dragged by but we enjoyed it we dressed back in our regular clothes and ran

up to go to lunch We had a great cafeteria staff Mrs. Ida Morrison always cooked a good

nutritious fare spaghetti was on the menu and it was good Tosha came up just as we were

leaving we stayed while she ate we walked out of the cafeteria there was an assembly

everyone went into the gym I sat down between April and Tosha. the principal walked up

and introduced several members of the armed forces they each spoke to us about the value

of serving our country several of the seniors went and talked to each recruiter I was

surprised and glad because I thought anyone brave enough to join during war time made

them extremely brave none of the teachers or principal tried to sway us one way or

another it must be our decision alone but I knew with what was happening in our family for now I couldn't even consider it by the time we were dismissed the school day had ended we went back to our lockers and we said our goodbyes I went out of the school in a much better frame of mind than when the day had started and I was thankful for that I was glad to find out how Grand's day had went she was in the car with Aunt Sophie I smiled and spoke Grand asked How my day was? I told her it was great and it was barring some unforeseen circumstances I talked with Susan she filled me in on her day, I noticed that Grand's color had returned to normal and I was elated we went into our bedroom and completed our homework Aunt Julie had prepared dinner it was good she made steak and cheese hoagies they were divine and we laughed and enjoyed our dinner we were told to turn in and we did just that, the next day got off to a roaring start we ate quickly we dressed and grabbed our backpacks we dropped off Susan first and then we went on to Westside the parking lot was full I said goodbye to my aunt and I got out and I walked to the front speaking to all that had chosen to speak to me. April and Tosha where in the cafeteria I ran over and sat at the table with them April said hi bestie I said hello darlings using my famous British accent we grabbed a fruit bowl and a juice we chatted and ate until the bell rang the morning went by so fast I was excited about going to Mrs. Russell's class I was excited walking into the Home Economics class always seemed to brighten my day because I loved to cook to create things that others would enjoy my mind was on high alert but that was not the case this day or I would have noticed Nicole's foot out in my path I stumbled I glanced back into her face with a look that told her I was tired of the games that they played I saw the huge smile on her face her eyes held a menacing sneer in the them I held my head high I wouldn't allow them to see the hurt and embarrassment they had caused me So I joined in the laughter Nicole said you're so basic! Mrs. Russell stood in front of the class and she said sweetly, enough of this rough housing. Nicole, I saw what you did and one more infraction of yours and you were sent directly to the principal's office but for today you have detention Nicole said, What? She said I'll not have another from you young lady she was a small statue of a woman but when she spoke you knew she had spoken and no one defied her I liked and admired her with all my heart she continued we are making omelets today we followed her over to the kitchen area she paired us all up she said Kimberly and Nicole a load moan came from Nicole she made a big show of gasping like she was deprived of oxygen she stomped her foot while she glared at us Mrs. Russell said take your things and go to the principal's office and you will not be allowed back in here for the rest of the semester for your outburst today I will not tolerate in subordinance Nicole she glanced at Carmen and said you can follow her if you wish! Carmen glanced down at her feet Mrs. Russell said I've wasted too much time on this nonsense I guess Kimberly you and April will partner up and Carmen you will work alone she walked over to one of the two individual counters April and I went over to our counter and washed our hands there was two slices of bacon and eggs some were given fruit we chopped up green peppers and onions we took out a frying pan and placed it on the stove April heated it up adding butter to the pan I whipped up the eggs and poured a thin layer in the pan the bacon was added to the pan it had cooked quickly the entire room smelled tantalizing. I used Mrs. Dash on our dish we each were given a small carton of orange juice we flipped the omelet over it had cooked well the eggs were golden my mouth was watering the timer went off by now everyone had taken their eggs out and had placed it on a platter I had added strawberries for a garnish April smiled and said you doing too much I smiled back at her and said I know right! Mrs. Russell came by each one of us with her fork. She took a small bite and she smiled after tasting the last pair. She said girls I am proud of you guys; you did a great job! We ate expeditiously and cleaned up our stations. She wrote on a piece of paper our grades we had received an A we hugged each other I gazed in Carmen's direction she had been a little too quick with her right hand she made a threatening gesture across her windpipe. I felt a slight chill crawl up my spine, but I would not give her the satisfaction that she had affected me in any manner Mrs. Russell said, class we will be making poached eyes and toast next class dismissed. April and I strolled from the room I could see Carmen rushing toward us we stepped into the hallway and I grabbed April's hand and we both darted out of sight glancing back I saw Carmen in the doorway frantically looking around for us I laughed and told April what our mad dash was all about I also told her of Carmen's classroom antics she said, No way! I said Yes way! We hi-fived stopping at our lockers to retrieve our biology books. and without haste we went directly to our class we took our seat we talked for a few minutes then the class was called to order, Our teacher stood at the front of the class with his glasses perched on the bridge of his nose, he said, I hope you studied your homework because today we are having a pop quiz several groans banded about the classroom he told us to clear off our desks everything but our number 2 pencils no pens were used in his class he always stated that if you couldn't do it with one then it couldn't be done. There were twenty questions in all I'm glad I had went over my reading assignment because it was manly pertaining to that with a few more thrown in for good measure April and finished at the same time we glanced at each other we both had very wide grins plastered on our faces I took our papers to the front April pulled out a romance novel she was so hooked on them forever believing in love I decided to work on some paperwork that was due in another class the next I always liked to stay ahead of the game

April commenting that she believed she had done well on the pop quiz I agreed with her April said we are so smart with a confidant smirk on her face I poked her in her side and she shamelessly giggled we exited the class and stopped off at our lockers I said I hope we have a fun activity in gym today she said me too we ran through the gym down to the locker room and we quickly changed our clothes.

Chapter 17

Our lockers were in the middle but where we were located, we considered a prime location up until now we rounded the locker, to the right and we saw Carmen and Nicole standing in front of the entrance, I felt anger flood my body. I said excuse me Carmen asked, you girls leaving so soon? I answered of course we are, Nicole said, Lesbos and Carmen whispered Bitches, and I answered and said it takes one to know one! Carmen whispered you too are so juvenile. I said maybe we are but then again, we are dealing with two children! She rushed over and shoved me into April, Nicole and Carmen crowded close together to block our exit I said to April this could turn ugly she frowned at me with fear in her eyes I heard the outer door open it was Mrs. Bundy she swiftly came into the room and glanced at us and said I was searching for you girls spending too much time in here will throw the class off. she glanced at Carmen and Nicole and asked is there a problem here? They said No, then let's go girls, she said I was silently glad she had shown up Mrs. Bundy put us on the trampoline none of it had escaped Mrs. Bundy she made them run laps around the gym April grabbed my hand she was shaking I glanced at her and said, it will be alright don't worry she took a deep breath and shook her head finding comfort in what I said I relaxed and allowed myself to enjoy on the trampoline I feel free as I jumped as high as I could after several moments April joined me and we laughed. Soon after a few more girls joined us with several staying on the floor to spot for us it was so much fun Mrs. Bundy announced that it was time to change we next went to the mats it wasn't long before I had forgotten about Carmen And Nicole last but not least we took turns on the high beam showers Mrs. Bundy said Carmen and Nicole I must speak privately with you she took them into her office we were dressed when they emerged from her office they were fuming and I was glad they deserved now if they could come to the conclusion to leave us alone April and I both would be relieved but that would be too much like right and I knew that they wouldn't give up that easy which made me sad because I didn't want to hurt or hurt anyone else they were making it harder to avoid the inevitable I would not let my guard down I would always have the workers in my brain to keep the mason sturdy and tight as I laughed to myself April asked Kimberly what are you laughing at I said oh nothing! her eyebrow arched like she didn't believe me, I decided against my better judgment to tell her after I finished she said I was worried about that situation also I told her I wasn't worried but never would I be unprepared again as a hardness set in she grabbed me by the arm and said enough of talking about them we went into the last class of the day and took our seats Tosha was already there we spoke but I noticed there was something off about her she was quiet and introverted there was something wrong and I meant to find out what it was the class was called to order one thing I loved about this class is it was always so busy that gave me very little time to ponder over my life and that mere thought made me happy. We were given a homework assignment Tosha said oh no I got plans later and asked doing what? She glanced just hanging out I said with who? For some reason that seemed to annoy her she became very evasive I decided to let it go for now I went on to talk about other things she soon brightened up I glanced at April she shrugged we went to our lockers and retrieved our books I was glad the day was over I could go home and check up on Grand we said goodbye to each other I ran out of the school I spotted my Aunt's car I was so happy when I saw Grand sitting beside her I got in Susan was busy with her homework I said Hi everyone replied in turn we drove off I pulled out my English homework soon my mind was engulfed in the essay I was working on Grand asked us about our day I let Susan take the lead and she soon had us laughing Grand said your awfully quite I said I have tons of homework she said that's good it will keep you busy. I said Grand, she said yes and we all giggled. My Aunt said girls were home. I put everything back in my backpack Grand said as we walked down the hall Kimberly don't worry about dinner we will prepare it I stopped and turned in her direction and asked are you sure? She smiled and went into the kitchen I felt such a relief come over me Grand strength was returning and I was so thankful I saw a twinkle in her eye no matter what I knew that the poison was meant to sicken her but what had saddened me was the fact that Mom had been involved even if she had no idea what Chris had planned but I knew he had a hidden agenda I must step up my efforts and keep my family safe after everyone had turned in for the night I went into the living room and checked the door and set the alarm and double checked all the windows I know you think I'm being a little too cautious but for some reason I didn't relax until I had accomplished this task I heard Susan call my name yes I said when I went back into our room she asked didn't you hear me Kimberly? I said yes I told her a little white lie I couldn't answer you I was having a tall glass of milk she said, I wish I would've known I would have had one too, I asked do you want me to accompany you to the kitchen she shook her head no I'm in the bed maybe next time I smiled at her and said yes next time I sat at my desk and completed my homework. The next day at school April asked me to meet her in the gym I arrived she was a little nervous I took a seat Mrs. Bundy smiled at me and said Kimberly the reason behind this impromptu meeting she scouted up to the desk resting her elbows and crossing her fingers in a thoughtful manner and said I want to take the volleyball team to state this year and I think you would be monumental in accomplishing that task, she looked me hard in the eye and asked So What do you think? I said well I'm shocked, but I say why not? You only live once and I glanced at April and said I will do anything I can to help Before I could finish April hugged me tightly honestly I was doing this for her because I knew this would make her extremely happy the coach told me that tryouts were today and the season only lasted 8 weeks I said ok I will be here April walked out in the hallway and told me thank you and I said there is no need it will be fun I imagine and to be honest I would rather be busy it gave me less time to think about my problems the rest of the day flew by I met up with Tosha and April after class and for some reason neither one of us mentioned the tryout to her I think April was starting to feel like something was off about her we bade her goodbye and ran off for tryouts April and I both got high marks and the judges chose us both so we were so very happy I had texted my Aunt so she knew I was staying after school. since they had lots of sizes I was asked my size and what number did I want to play with I said number ten because I tried to be the best in everything I did the teams had been given new equipment so everyone was excited there was a small few that didn't make the team but they were still kept as extras and no one seemed to mind I was glad when I got into the car I held up my uniform and Grand said wow my girl is good at all sports I said not all she smiled and said don't fault me because I'm overjoyed for you we rode home with everyone in high spirits Susan leaned close to me and whispered your great at everything I said stop girl and she start to giggle I had always liked volleyball but I was so engrossed in Cheerleading and basketball I hadn't given it much thought but at the end of the day I was going to give it all that I got! Grand made a special dinner to celebrate we had steak and potatoes it was so good Susan was so bubbly it was contagious we all started to laugh the steak was so flavorful and tender I piled lots of sour cream on top of my potatoes and dug in Susan said

Grand you outdid yourself Grand smiled and said I always do we snickered my Aunt I noticed hadn't had much to say since picking me up that in itself was weird, I finished my meal and Susan and I cleaned the kitchen while they went into the living room to relax after such a hefty meal Susan went in and started on her homework. Grand called me from her room I went in and she told me to shut the door when I glanced at her I felt a severe pain in my gut I knew whatever she had to say was not going to be good I braced myself she said Kimberly your mother wants to move back in with Chris in your house and I told her that was impossible after what he did she said they are homeless and she doesn't want to be on the street Grand, I said No! No! Grand isn't there something we can do? We mustn't let them at this point. I don't trust either of them! I stood up and stepped away from Grand's bed, she said Kimberly I understand how you feel, she cleared her throat and walked toward me taking me in her arms I started to tremble she said dear, holding me gently in her arms Kimberly please understand the dilemma I am in make no mistake about it I feel exactly as you do but she is my daughter I love her and if something happens to her and I could of done something to prevent it I will never be able to forgive myself, after all she is your Mother shaking my head I said I don't care Grand I feel as though it is us against them and after what they did I cannot fathom how you could ask me that, Grand took a deep breath and sat back down on the bed her face was pale gathering my wits I rushed over and said Grand are you ok? She answered yes, I am! But I could tell she was telling me that so that I wouldn't worry about her I closed my eyes and stared at her I could feel myself caving in. I said Grand I will stand behind your decision, if I feel threatened in any manner I will call the police, your Mom has asked you girls to move back in with her a wave of nausea soon overcame me by law I have to consider her request, but that doesn't mean I can't accompany you I hugged her and said thank you Grand shrugged and said we will make it through this, smiling I said I'm glad you believe we will! I got up and walked out of her room and closed the door standing there for a minute to compose myself I went into the kitchen my Aunt and Susan were talking she was bringing Susan up to speed she got from the table and ran over and started to hug me I grasped her face looking down into her eyes I said Susan it will be fine we haven't got a choice but Grand will be moving in with us again our Aunt added so will I we glanced at her I knew I had to be strong for everyone especially Susan, No matter what he will not break this family I said, my mouth said one thing but inside my mind was a swirl of emotions I thought of an old saying, never let them see you sweat! I had to keep them all safe Grand was still recovering My Aunt made eye contact with me over Susan's head I knew she was thinking the same thing I was I said hey kiddo we better go get started on our homework she said I will race you we ran into our room laughing I sat at the desk and she climbed onto the bed without further ado we opened our books? Both of us had strong work ethics we worked for several hours I finally closed my book Susan was already in the shower I followed suit without any fuss I think we were shocked at the turn of events I quickly showered I was tired this thing with my Mom was very frustrating I laid In my bed looking at the ceiling I thought over the entire thing for the life of me I couldn't shake the feeling that Chris was behind this sudden change of heart I knew if it was his idea then he had a plan of that I was sure What did he want? Mom followed blindly behind him and if this what love was then I wanted no part of it. I silently said my prayers. I had to reassure Grand that I was happy about this. I had no idea how I would pull that off but I had to try. I came awake to my Aunt saying Kimberly it's time to get up. I answered already. She laughed and said Yes already! Susan was still asleep I woke her on my way to the bathroom I went in I brushed my teeth and washed my face quickly getting dressed I went into the dining room I was greeted by Grand's laughter after Susan joined us I felt the energy in the room as I ate my breakfast we all seemed to be in a much lighter mood finally realizing that we had been waiting for gauntlet to drop and now that it has we were glad it was over I don't know about them but I definitely was I would rather know than not it was relieving to feel this way, and if we had to face this monster then we would do it together. And there was always strength in numbers. I grabbed my backpack and headed out to the car they were urgently waiting for, I got in and asked Waiting for me? With a smirk on my face Grand said really. I said really and we all laughed, I was dropped first because they had to go to talk to the office about her schedule I said bye you guys, I jumped out and walked into the school I ran into April and Tosha at our lockers they were debating over some subject or other no one to miss out on anything I quickly joined in April was talking about the fiasco at the white house she was saying she hated what the country was going through right now Tosha was on the president's side about the border wall I said I will be glad when this is over there are so many families that are going without getting paid April said I know it is sad but I understand both sides of the aisle I said I don't they can build the wall if they want but not at the expense of families going without Tosha went on the defensive and Listened for a time but I realized she wasn't making any sense we were all republicans but more than that we were Americans and I was proud to be one. Ladies Grand always told me never to bring up politics or religion Tosha asked Why? I said with a smirk Because no one ever agrees and it's sure to cause an argument, April said I agree Tosha glanced at us with a serious nod she said Girls I'm off to class April said see you later.

Chapter 18

I watched her and I knew in my gut there was something off about her, April asked what's wrong Kimberly I said I don't know but it's just a feeling I grabbed her arm and we went to class the morning was a total flurry with exams in all my morning classes by the time I walked into the gym I was more than ready to blow off some steam after the class I had a meeting with Mrs. Bundy I sprinted out her office and I placed my purse and phone in my locker and noticing the time I had to hurry I raced to the shower I heard a locker open and close in the distance as I turned the nozzle on I stood there and reached for my shower gel l lathered myself and rinsed myself off my mind was million miles away I didn't hear Carmen and Nicole when they slipped up behind me someone grabbed my arm while the other one placed a page over my head I struggled my arms failing this way and that I started to scream my sound was muffled by the bag something hit me in the center of my back I fought back with everything in me I heard someone calling my name it was a familiar voice Tosha, so her true self was right there for all to see that bitch, she said you and April couldn't of possible thought I wanted to be your friend you bitches are so gullible she snickered happily I was unable to breathe I knew it would be moments before I lost consciousness extreme weakness came over me my hands were restrained I thrashed and kicked this went on for a minute or two then the bag was yanked off my head I heard them running off as I gasped for breath. I collapsed onto the shower room floor laying there for a second. I pulled myself up and came to my knees that's when I heard the locker room door open Mrs. Bundy yelled loudly Kimberly , did you get lost in here? Breathing heavily when she rounded the bend she ran over and gathered me in my arms she asked what happened? Are you alright? Nothing I answered I slipped and fell there were bruises beginning to surface on both of my arms she helped me up and wrapped me in my towel she walked me to my locker I sat on the bench she suddenly said Kimberly I know that something happened and I believe I have a pretty good idea of who did this to you and for the life I don't know why you are trying to protect them because without your cooperation my hands are tied throwing her hands in the air in a frustrating manner she walked allowing me to get dressed I grabbed my backpack and headed out the door she ran up to me and gave me a tardy slip to give to my next class I thanked her she assured me that she was going to investigate this and she would never let this happen in her class again I briefly hugged her and walked out of the gym I called April she said she was standing in front of our lockers talking with Tosha I said wait for me I'm on my way April asked where have you been I've been looking for you I said I know I will explain when we are alone she said ok without going into detail. April was smiling at something Tosha was saying she grabbed me by the shoulder I winced as the pain radiates down my entire arm April removed her hand concern written all over face but because of our previous conversation she didn't question me I was glad I glanced at Tosha there was a sparkle in her eyes and somehow I knew she was aware of what had happened. I swallowed and smiled. I had to keep this tidbit to myself I engaged her in our conversation and since she didn't know me well there, she thought I was clueless and until I found out more, she needed to be kept in the dark. I walked in the middle of them my arms around both of their shoulders drawing them close while we strolled to the last class of the day the teacher call the class to order and we were given a worksheet pertaining to the homework assignment we had been given April whispered I'm glad I did mine but I could tell by the facial expressions of some of the other student they hadn't I winked at her and the teacher noticed our exchange she said April you and Kimberly focus your attention on your what's in front you I said Yes Ma'am and snickers could be heard from across the room after a moment or two my mind was in engrossed on my work and I was too busy to join in with them ignoring Tosha she was lightly tapping her foot against my desk she annoyed me more and more each day and I had no known reason to react this way towards her. but I couldn't seem to stop myself I closed my eyes open the red room door a crack storing those thoughts in there for later I sat up straighter in my chair reminding me of the quandary I had been in earlier visibly shaking my head achieving excellent grades was first and foremost other than my family I finished my paper in record time and handed it in and I wrote down my homework assignment for tonight actually I was ecstatic the more I had to do the less time I had to ponder over my many dilemmas between Mom and Chris and Carmen and her entourage I had no idea which was more vexing. Class was soon over Tosha said she was meeting her Mom for an appointment April and I were in our lockers when I heard Carmen voice her and Nicole came really near us and stopped and asked we were concerned about your injury you had in the gym I turned around quickly and confronted them and said you two are bitter attention seeking Ho's and guess what you are only sixteen imagine that! I started laughing even though it hurt me and was very sore and swollen in several areas. They briskly walked away but not before giving me the middle finger April asked me what was that all about I told her what had happened and she leaned back against the locker clutching her stomach I wrung my hands I walked in front of my locker facing away from her and took a deep breath I turned and faced her gathering my resolve silently I prayed and asked God to help me I wasn't strong enough and I couldn't do it without me, I stared her deep in her eye and then I said April I am fine don't worry. April said this is getting out of hand we must tell somebody we cannot let them continue to do this to us I replied I know, I know, I'm going to take care of this you hear me she turned toward and said yes Kimberly but I am scared of them, I said but I'm not and I will not allow them to bother you I gently said to her look I have to go, she hugged me and we stood there for a second before we walked out of the school arm and arm. I rushed off jumping into the car with my Aunt and Susan said Hi Kim then I heard My Aunt say they are fine no need to worry ok, the more she talked I thought it was Grand but then I started to feel a sense of dread she pushed the speaker on her phone my Mom said Kimberly Susan I miss you guys so very much I whispered to my Aunt to hang up she stared at me I stared out the window then I laid my head back and closed my eyes my day had been overwhelming as it is and I didn't have an inkling of sympathy in my body to indulge my Mother we backed out and the conversation continued for another ten minutes or so by the time she finally hung up the phone I was livid My Aunt asked me if I was ok I answered Yes I'm just tired but even to my own ears my voice sounded mousy for once the car was extremely quiet with everyone deep within the depths of their own mind. Grand met us at the door she spoke to us then Aunt Sophie took her off to the kitchen while we went in our room minutes later Susan gave me a smile and started in on her homework I walked out of the room and Grand and Aunt Sophie were at the table conversing and having a cup of coffee she suddenly asked me Kimberly dear you look distraught I sat at the table with them I talked to them almost non-stop about what had occurred in gym Aunt Sophie jumped up angrily and said Oh my God! Grand was shocked her face was as white as a sheet she asked me again was I ok she came over and ran into her arms her arms tightened around me I winced she pulled my shirt up my arms and the bruises were vivid in dark blue and purple hues she almost collapsed. Aunt Sophie and I helped her to her

seat she was shaking I realized I had to hide my hurt and pain and bare it for Grand's sake I

mustn't falter I had to be strong for her but deep inside I needed someone to be strong for

me I said over and over that I was fine Grand told me to go and run some bath water she

went into her bathroom and gave a bag of Epsom salt told me to use have a cup in my water

and go soak in water and it would remedy my pain somewhat I hugged each of them and

went back into my room I ran the bath and poured the Epsom into the water I added some

bubble bath and closed the door I stripped and I tested the water to make sure the water

wasn't too hot I lowered myself into the water and heat and the aroma soothed me I soaked

until the water cooled off I let the water out and ran the shower I stayed in there for over

an hour by the time I came out I felt more like myself and I felt totally refreshed I grabbed

my dirty clothes placing them into the hamper Susan was no longer in the room I smelled

something good coming from the kitchen I stood in front of the mirror and said to myself

that I couldn't allow them to win suddenly laughing at my reflection I ran into dining room

Grand had recovered her and Aunt Sophie had prepared dinner and it looked scrumptious

Grand said Kimberly you have a seat Susan had already set the table and was busy pouring

our drinks without any arguments from me I sat back and waited patiently for my plate.

Grand filled it up to the brim and I was happy because I was hungry. Susan sat down next to

me and Grand led us In prayer and we commenced to eating. We were all in a better frame

of mind and for this I was delighted. We laughed and chatted about the closeness of family

is what I needed. I was glad that it was Friday because I knew I needed time away from the

school and from Carmen and Nicole time to get thoughts in order I glanced at Susan she

was happy acting more like a child without worries if I could keep all of the world nastiness from her I would do so in reality I couldn't spare her from it all but as much of that I could keep from our doorstep I would. Today's fiasco crossed my mind over and over again I had to find a way to eliminate the problem without harm coming to me or April. I had to find a way to get control of the situation because I had been taking their crap for some time and the things that they did now were at the point of the most extreme Susan walked by me and I grabbed her and wrestled her on the bed for a couple of seconds I laid on my side while she while she plummeted me with a couple of her punches. She asked me Kimberly , don't you feel well. I said yes pumpkin I feel fine, it's just been a long day it wasn't entirely the truth I wasn't tired it was more mental than physical I knew I had to get out of the funk that I was in. So, I jumped up and went into the kitchen Aunt Sophie said I was just about to call you dear, how are you? I said if someone asks that question one more time, I am going to scream. She smiled and said ok, I'll leave you alone for now I shrugged, and she said in a flip tone bye girl! We giggled and Grand having heard our conversation she walked into the kitchen and said, I don't know what I'm going to do with you guys! I smiled at her and answered I don't know Grand, maybe just keep us. She grinned from ear to ear and said, Why I think I will. I hugged them and exited the room I laid across my bed that's when I started to relax I prayed and soon after I was asleep, I woke up with one of Grand's quilts covering me with a renewed sense of vigor I jumped up and went into to the bathroom I relieved myself and jumped into the shower the bruises were covering the upper portion of my body but other than that I felt more like my old self I totally enjoyed the heat and the freshness that radiated while I toweled myself off I brushed my teeth and when I opened the door Susan was still fast asleep not wanting to awaken her I closed the door quietly and I went to help Grand prepare our breakfast, Good morning Grand she said good morning dear get the carton of eggs out and crack four eggs in a bowl and crack six in a separate bowl the smaller for French toast the bigger amount for scrambled eggs I said yes ma'am and swished by her she patted me on my bottom and I said Oww, she said yeah right.And we both laughed aloud and were still in high spirits when Susan and Aunt Sophie joined us, she told me to have a seat and smiled as I did. One thing this family was known for babying the one in need and I better enjoy this while I could I thought smiling to myself Grand said grace and we dug in without further ado Susan and I both had a double helping of French toast it was so buttery and good and we all thoroughly enjoyed our breakfast I jumped up but Aunt Sophie said Kimberly I will wash the dishes I said no I got this and Susan followed and helped me I washed and she dried the dishes and put them away while Grand went into the den and watched one of her many programs I grimaced at Susan and she laughed and said we are quite the team I answered and said I know right! Deciding amongst ourselves to clean the entire house except their bedrooms Susan dusted the living room and den while I ran the vacuum Grand said you girls are certainly diligent I said we sure are, laughing joyously Susan tackled the hallway bathroom while Iast but not least I went and cleaned our room she ran into the bathroom and assisted me with the shower walls and tub when we finally finished we sat on our beds with all the activity I hadn't even noticed the soreness in my arms which goes to show that when you are in pain you can put it in the back of your mind sometimes if it is not too extreme but after that thought quickly I felt the pain return I washed my hands again and lotioned them and I climbed back under the covers to rest for a while quite soon descended upon the room, maybe a little to quite! Grand stuck her head in the room to see what we were up to she said I was just going to suggest that you do exactly that, glancing at us no matter what we did it would be very hard to fool her, we think alike smirking she said, tapping her finger on her chin I said uhm and closed my eyes to avoid her probing stare she briefly sat on the edge of the bed and asked if I was sure I was fine I shook my head to reassure her Susan had her head phones on so I whispered Grand don't worry I am fine and I will soon heal, Grand had a knack for not knowing when to let go but I knew this and in her condition I must be patient with her I reached up and hugged her then I felt Susan eyes on me that's when I truly realized she was aware that I needed space and she was attempting to give me some I grabbed one of my pillows and threw it at her after grand left we had a pillow fight to end all pillow fight both us were out rand of breath and sweating profusely smiling and sense of peace came over me and I laid across my bed and closed my eyes and thought to myself I will just lay here for a few minutes and before I knew I was snoring Susan silently watched me before succumbing to it herself. Grand allowed us to sleep pass lunchtime waking us right near dinner time we got up and went into the kitchen with Grand's gay chatter leading the way the phone rang Grand left me in charge of stirring the homemade chili she answered the phone then took it to her room to talk in private Susan said I bet it's Mom I said.

Chapter 19

I'm sure it is Aunt Sophie came out of her room having heard some of the conversation from her room she looked as exasperated as I felt. Grand reappeared close to a half an hour later she went into the den and took a seat on the couch. We all solemnly joined her, and I blurted out Grand what did she want? She took a long breath and said Kimberly and Susan your Mom wants us to move back into the house with her and she said if you don't want to stay then she will not object, Susan glanced at me with tears glistening in her eyes, more than anything I didn't want her to be hurt but I knew she was miserable without Mom, I stared hard into Grand's eyes and said ok Grand we will give her another chance we love her and all we want is for it to workout. Grand stared back. She was listening to me but wholeheartedly she was aware of my true feelings, but I had to bury them deep within myself and do this for Susan because I will not add to her pain. I turned to Susan and grabbed her and held her in my arms while she silently wept. Grand came over and we sat like that for some time Grand gathered us both in her arms I drew strength from her finally we went into our room baby girl if need me I will always be here for you she smiled and she said I'm tired she plopped down on her bed I needed a reprieve I went into the bathroom and closed the door I whispered to myself I am tired too. I took a quick shower standing under the water as it cascaded down my body truth be told I was scared a deep sense of gloom prickled like a chill all over my body there was a unknown reason why my Mom wanted us to come stay with her it matters not that she claimed to miss us I wasn't doubting that but she had changed and the more I tried to find her the woman that she use to be it become harder and harder if I saw the a thread of the person I knew her to be I would be all in but she lies and her whole life is full of hidden agendas trust is not something that I will give away freely to her because she would have to earn it and I refused to make it easy for her I turned the faucet off and stepped out of the shower for Susan I must try and I hoped and prayed that some of the woman that had raised us still remained thinking these thoughts saddened me because I needed my Mom but if her actions are not pure I will not deal with it. Dressing quickly in my pajamas I came out of the bathroom with Susan quickly going in to Grand's room, Grand I called loudly, she answered Yes, dear standing by the door with her arms folded with a smile on her face I asked if she was in the mood to watch a western she said sure I am do you want to join me I said yes linking my arm in hers leading her away from the door quietly I went into the kitchen and popped us some kettle corn and poured us each a tall glass of tea Grand grabbed us a coaster while changing the channel to the western network I smiled and plopped down on the couch next to her. We soon were engrossed in the movie it had a great story line but it was one we had seen before my mind was a jumble of emotions I couldn't seem to concentrate my thoughts were on our struggles and the undying love we had for each other mind you I wasn't delusional there were some families that seem to have no issues and others had more than their fair share. And ours was the latter more than the former Grand hugged me. I laid my head on her shoulders elated at her comfort. We sat like that for some time, actually I started to relax, Grand said Kimberly you had better turn in for the night, I glanced at Grand and answered yes ma'am! She opened her mouth to say she wasn't a ma'am but I beat her to the punch we both laughed gleefully I jumped up and ran to my room leaving her in total shock she expected me to try wiggle out of it, but not tonight I was sleepy I went into my room and found Susan fast asleep I walked over giving her a quick peck on her forehead and I climbed into bed without thought I said my prayers and minutes later I was asleep. Morning came swiftly a little to swiftly to me we ate Grand kept watching me I plastered a smile on not wanting anyone to worry about me, Aunt Sophie said girls we are leaving soon so make sure to pack enough for a few days, neither one of us said anything Susan went to get her things together I sat at the table knowing that if I lingered longer it would only delay the inevitable. but a sense of foreboding had seeped into my pores and I was terrified but I had no real reason to be I didn't believe my Mother would try to hurt but I had no real proof that she wouldn't I disliked being in an quandary dislike it or not it was dilemma that I was faced with Grand had eased behind me she laid her hands on my shoulders and asked me if I was going to be alright? I said yes I am Don't concern yourself I will be with you girls I think Sophie will be going home for a few days I glanced at her with a skeptical look upon my face we must work together to insure your safety I asked if you don't trust her then why are we going again? Grand answered and said Kimberly one day you will have children then you will understand how I feel she is my child and I love her and I hope somewhere deep inside of her she will remember that Logically the same thoughts were b behind the façade I presented for the entire world but I couldn't fool her she knew I was devastated by Mom's behavior something about this whole thing was off and Grand hands were shaking slightly I touched her gently and said we will manage no matter what the outcome will be we always do, Kimberly said Susan come here, I said loudly I'm on my way, I winked at Grand the closeness of family is the only thing that kept the terror at bay the severity of that thought was cemented in my mind. When you don't want to leave the time passes so very fast we packed the cars Aunt Sophie would trail us home I thank God for dear Susan because her constant chatter helped us I talked as diligently as I could, Grand drove at her normal speed even she was quite that's when I truly realized how worried she really was, I brightened up the Doctor said no stress, so I knew it was all up to me I engaged them both Grand was soon laughing her sweet laughter was music to my ears Grand pulled into our driveway and before anyone could come to grips with what we were about to embark on Mom opened the door and came outside she looked terrible like she had been through hell and back Grand gasped, I said we are here now things will get better Susan said I hope so she got out and ran to Mom engulfed her in a big hug we all did the same we stood liked that for several minutes.

Chapter 20

I said Grand you and Mom go on we will get the bags out of the car they both said ok Grand was openly staring at my Mother like she was an alien I felt almost sorry for her Aunt Sophie had silently slipped away after she had observed our reunion, That's when I noticed that Susan was quietly crying I held her smoothing her hair gently praying that what I was doing helped her in some way we stood out there beside the car for several moments until she gathered herself together I lightly kissed her on her cheek and said I love you kiddo she smiled we reached and grabbed two bags apiece Susan said thank you Kimberly for always being there for me I replied that my dear will never change I opened the door and she went before me and I followed close behind her Susan said Oh no as she looked around the room I dropped the bags loudly and slowly began to back up until I came in contact with wall beside the front door the living room was in complete chaos there was clothes all over the room the kitchen had dishes piled high in the sink the dust on the tables was so thick our house looked unrecognizable Grand was at the table with her mouth gaped open in utter shock I asked aloud Mom how could you let our house go to pot? she was sitting in her chair shaking Grand suddenly said, ok girls let's get to work and restore this place we took our bags to our individual rooms and they hadn't been touched I was glad for that I headed for the kitchen and Susan went into the living room Grand said you know better, as she glanced at her daughter shaking her head Grand started a load of clothes while Mom cleaned the bathrooms we cleaned the house from top to bottom I saw the fatigue in Grand's face and I said Grand why don't you take a breather we will finish up I even started dinner I defrosted a chicken and I cleaned and seasoned it I put on a pot of pasta and fresh spinach Grand came into the kitchen asking if I needed her help, I said no you rest she shook her slightly as she poured herself a cup of fresh coffee and she said thank you Kimberly you know I needed this I said I know right! She answered right and we smiled Mom came in and said Steve will not be back neither one of us responded, deep down I was so glad for Grand because without her I don't know that I could do this I asked Mom is this why you wanted us back here to clean Mom said no Kimberly I missed you girls I said sure you did! Grand said Kimberly lay off it's been hard on us all, but I will say this if you are playing some asinine game you will live to regret it without a backward glance she stalked off to her room. I was so glad that Grand had put it so bluntly and there would be no room for a misrepresentation I stared at Mom trying my best to make her feel as uncomfortable as I did I prepared dinner and then went and retrieved the rest of the family Susan set the table while I made some tea Susan observed me and said Kimberly don't forget the lemons I said I wasn't planning on it munchkin! Mom came in to join us after Grand had said grace, we continued to talk with only Susan acknowledging her presence Susan with her bubbly attitude soon had us all laughing, she winked at me not one for confrontations she squealed and muttered your eyes are twinkling she got up and went around the table and hugged Mom tears sprang to my eyes Grand said we may not be able to turn back the clock but we can make new wonderful memories smiling at us all I said hear! hear! Our meal was indeed scrumptious with everyone except Mom wanting a second helping, Susan and I cleaned the kitchen while Grand and Mom talking quietly, Grand didn't want to alarm us but I decided not to wear my headphones so most of the conversation I was able to hear Grand sounded aggravated I think she was tired of listening to Mom because to be honest everything that had occurred was not all of Chris's fault some of it was

Mom's she was aware that we were all disappointed in her when we went to bed they were still talking Grand wouldn't give up on her daughter Susan and I kissed them both and said goodnight, she came into my room and we chatted for a few moments, Susan said, I'm going to take a shower and go to sleep I said me too kiddo! I pulled my hair up into a scrunchie and began taking off my clothes Susan, I said if you need me for anything don't hesitate to come and sleep in here, she bucked her eyes and said, you are a worry wart Kimberly, I smiled and said someone has to be munchkin! She grinned and flounced out of my room I undressed and went in the bathroom and took my shower I truly loved my bathroom the shower head was adjustable I stayed in there for as long as humanly possible when I emerged from the shower I felt as though all my issues and problems had been washed down the drain and I knew no matter what I could master anything that was thrown in my path. There was a knock on my door hurriedly I dressed and got under the covers and said come in, it was my Mom she asked may I come in? I said sure she closed the door. I said abruptly I'm sleepy. Can we make this quick! Not being able to fathom at this point why she wanted to talk to me alone she glanced around the room and she said simply, I am glad that you guys came home she went off into a long monolog I listened attentively at first but the more she talked it was almost like she preparing me for something. I suddenly interrupted her, and asked Mom is Chris coming back? Never once making eye contact with me she said in a soft voice, not that I know of, something about this whole fiasco was suspicious and that feeling of dread that I tried to keep hidden rose to the surface like a volcano about to erupt.

a cold chill ran down my spine as though someone had just walked over my grave. She walked over to the door and said I hope one day you can forgive me her response went unanswered I grabbed my phone and texted Susan to check on her she texted me back and said she was listening to music, placing my ear buds in I got on YouTube immersing myself not realizing that Mom had unlocked the inside latch to the window in the hallway bathroom Grand had long since turned in for the night she was fast asleep in her room Mom had laced her tea with several melatonin one was indeed enough to knock out the average person. Chris had convinced Mom that he couldn't bear to be parted from her and she had bought that pile of bull without a contradiction. The house soon quitted down with everyone asleep not wanting to break protocol I got up and decided to do my nightly check of the house I crept out of my room closing the door behind me, I stood there for a second so that my eyes could adjust to the darkness but at the end of the hallway I saw a tall hulking figure standing in front of my Susan's room my eyes widened with fear a silvery glint flashed in the dark it was a long dagger the unknown assailant was swaying back and forth like he was a wave in the ocean I gasped my hand going to my mouth he walked into the dim light that when I recognized his familiar gait it was Chris, Oh My God! What was he doing here? I asked myself he silently placed a finger up to his mouth, his hair was all over his head and his eyes were bloodshot his lips were snarling like a rabid dog spittle was foaming at the corners of his mouth he appeared mad like a fiend I had concocted from one of my many horror movies, I stared at him his hand went to the door handle shaking my head no please I couldn't allow him to hurt Susan I raced over grabbing his hand revulsion running all through my body I lead him away from her door and I walked pass the bathroom and went back into my room I stood there he followed me in shutting the door his chest heaved and he started laughing without making a sound I said I knew you and Mom had a plan but I never believed she could be so depraved you are a different story he wiped his mouth and said look bitch you had better watch your mouth before I change my

mind and take this party to your little sister's room I imagine she would enjoy my company

my bravado went my body went into overload I daydreamed all my life about meeting my

knight in shining amour and us riding away into the sunset to live happily ever after I had

saved my virginity for this slug of a man maybe I could get out of this but I rationalized that

there was only one way out I had to go through with this if it would protect Susan I must do

this monstrous deed he locked my door and placed the knife on my night stand fear was

not an option I swallowed hard all my hurt and pain a vision of myself was perpetrating

this act not my true self my hand shook as I unbuttoned my pajama top I closed my eyes

while I opened it I slid my pants down my hips and stepped out of them I braced myself and

stood with a regal bearing opening my eyes, his face was a blaze with desire he licked like

he was about to partake of a delicious meal, he watched me for a trace of apprehension he

needed it if I was to play this game It had to be played right I let my guard down and I cried

and I dropped down to the floor he whispered yes, yes he reached down and rubbed his

penis violently as he continued to lose control, he said Daddy is going to give you a treat I

wanted to vomit to empty my stomach right there on the carpet but I knew I couldn't so I

sat there staring off into the abyss he yanked me to my feet and shoved me on to the bed he

stared down at me and pulled his shirt over his head unfastened his belt he stood before

me naked he was sweating he smelled real bad like he hadn't had a bath in days he said you

have a beautiful body coming from him it sounded like an insult he pulled my legs apart so

savagely a pain resonated in my very center I screamed he claimed on top of me I said put

on a condom because if you don't and I become pregnant I will alert law enforcement he

said girl if you do I will hurt everyone in this house starting with Susan I started to shake but I must have gotten through to him because he climbed back off and went into his pocket and pulled one out and rolled one onto his swollen penis it was dripping with a white cream ugh it resembled puke then I said I have one last thing to say he said speak I roughly said, if you go anywhere near my sister I will kill you he snickered like a child he glanced at me deeply in my eyes and said with a sneer you are one crazy bitch but I felt a small sense of gratification for my eyes mirrored my truth! One of his snarly hands grabbed my left breast he pinched me so hard he left a bruise mark there leaning so close to my face I thought he was going to kiss me thank God that was not the case rubbing me roughly between my legs he said snidely you dry as an old hag he position his penis over me and before I had a chance to think he thrust into me I could feel the tearing of my flesh he yelled out aloud my fingers dug into the sheets beneath me the pain was so severe I thought I would pass out I saw stars shooting out from my very lids I bite the inside of inner jaw I could the blood flowing into my mouth he moved in and out of me not once slowing down I laid there in my bed but somehow I must retreat people sometimes tell you when you are unable to deal find your happy place and that is exactly what I did I imagined myself walking on a white sandy beach with the sun high overhead and the water gently lapping at my feet I reached into the water it was so incredibly clear and pristine I saw dolphins in the distance jumping in and out of the water it was so peaceful and beautiful that's when I was shaken by Chris he said you were wonderful when can we do this again that's when I looked up at him with a blank face I reached under my pillow and grabbed the pair of scissors that I kept there and jab him into his neck not very deep or so I thought because he yelped like a wounded animal and rolled off of me and slid on the floor I jumped up noticing the blood on the sheet and a sticky stream of blood between my legs I grabbed a kotex pad from my lower drawer and pulled on a fresh pair of pajama pants and I rolled

him up in my bed sheets my mind was racing what should I do? I ran into my shower

wanting to get his touch and smell off of me as the water flowed over my body the blood

went down the drain along with my innocence I stood there and cried until I couldn't cry

any longer I came out of the shower and when I opened the door the first thing I saw was

his body I got dressed and went into the garage and grabbed a large piece of plastic that

Mom normally kept there then it suddenly hit me why hadn't we woke up my Mom, always

in the past she would have come out of her room to see what the problem was, I tried to be

as quite as I could I opened my door and quickly rolled Chris on the plastic and I rewrapped

his body in the sheet, I had to get rid of him I decided to put him in the lake that was behind

our house there was a ravine I could use to my advantage I used the cart we had in the

garage I placed him on it and I dressed in dark clothes I must hurry, I dragged him off the

cart and placed him on the edge of the tree line and pushed him he slid down the ravine

and he went into the water I stood there and watched him sink into the dark murky water,

breathing a ragged sign of relief I walked slumped over back to our house and I made sure

no one was following me before I entered the rear entry of the garage I made sure everyone

was sleep checking my Mom's room last she was wide awake lying on the bed I stood over

her for several minutes before she opened her eyes there was fear mirrored there she

never asked me what I was doing, standing over her in the dark I said with complete malice

in my voice, I knew you were awake you let that monster in and allowed him to do

unspeakable things to me she stared at me but not once did she deny these allegations I

told her in cause her conscience did resurface at a later date I recorded the entire thing so if

you think for a minute you are going to turn me in, Kimberly I wouldn't do that to you he threatened to kill us all I had to do that she said, shut up Mother I'm tired of your flimsy

excuses she flushed a deep red a hand shakily covering her mouth I seriously felt sorry for

her she said I am truly sorry I bought him into our lives that's when I glanced around the

room her room had been remodeled she had purchased a whole new bedroom she sat up

and I ran into her arms and I stayed in that position for a long time I cried myself to sleep

when I awaken I was tucked in beside her the sun was bright suddenly remembering the

thing I had done my insides were tied in knots I sat on the side of the bed I ran my hands

through my hair and that's when the door burst open and it was Susan she threw herself on

Mom and said if I was kept out of the a family slumber party I'm gonna extremely mad with

a huge grin on her face the sight of her melted my heart and while hugging her Grand called

us in for breakfast we went in I noticed that Grand and Mom were embracing but before we

sat down Grand said, Not at my table you girls go and wash those dirty faces we ran and did

just that Grand said the blessing we ate and chatted Mom watched me closely I didn't want

my guilt to show but with each joke I told and every laugh that I took I felt it breakfast

lasted longer than usual but we soon got up and went and bathed and got dressed for

church I was anxious to go we had missed Sunday school but we arrived just in time for the

service the pastor noticed us and acknowledge us and he spoke on being happy that Grand

was better and looked as fit as a fiddle one of her saying not mine's the service was about

the Ten Commandments, and how we must not break them thou shall not kill I felt like he

was talking to me like he knew what I had done and it went on and on I had never felt

uncomfortable in church but this time I did, and it must of shown on my face because Mom

grabbed my hand and she held it tightly the emotions were so overwhelming It felt like I

was being consumed, I took a deep breath that's when, Grand turned and observed us I couldn't fess up to her on the actuality of the matter, but I had to come up with a story that would suffice for now attempting a smile she frowned at me all my life I had found it hard to lie to her and this time would be no different. Time seemed to drag on for hours finally we stood on our feet for the dismissal prayer.

Chapter 21

  Honestly I was glad the service was over Grand and Mom greeted several people that they hadn't seen for some time Susan and I waited for them, I asked Susan Did she want to go outside? she said sure Kimberly we proceeded to do just that we walked to the car and jumped up on the truck and sat down Susan went off into one of her stories about her friends I listened solemnly to her she suddenly asked Kimberly what is wrong with you? You don't seem like yourself. I smirked and asked with as much gusto as I could muster munchkin, how would you? Susan winked broadly at me and said trust me I know! Grand and Mom listened to the end of the conversation they were standing by the back passenger door Grand walked around the back to the back of the car and she said, Kimberly I know that there is something wrong with you and when we get home we are going to talk I glanced at her and sure we must, thinking to myself there would be no more evading I had to tell her...... we rode in complete silence no one uttering a single word by the time we arrived home Grand went into her room and I obediently followed her before she even had a chance to call me she placed her purse on the bed and she said close the door she reached into her pill box and she swallowed a small pill It was her nitroglycerin allowing her time to catch her bearing I decided to tread carefully she turned and faced me my palms started to sweat I said, Grand I killed Chris after he raped me Grand pallor turned white I sunk to my knees in front of her she whispered Kimberly it will be alright we will get through this, don't worry she asked me where is his body? I told her where It was without leaving out any details, Grand was shaken but it was only for my sake. but I felt a sense of relief come over me she held me I cried until I was spent when we finally did emerge from the bedroom mom and Susan had prepared dinner we sat down to dinner Grand said Kimberly lead us in prayer, I was afraid but we had been taught that if you ever do anything wrong God would always forgive you, so I hung my head my voice trembled I said Thank you Mighty God for this bounty you have blessed us with and I ask for your forgiveness where we fall short in Jesus mighty name we pray, Grand said well done, she passed me the meat platter I took a slice and passed it on, thank God for Susan she kept us entertained I ate because I knew all eyes were on me I had to choke down every bite my mouth was like the Sierra Desert dry, but I managed to do so Mom said, Kimberly we are going to clean the kitchen why don't you go and rest for a while I glanced at her and said, I believe I will, I walked to my room my hand was on the doorknob when Grand said Kimberly come here please, I almost raced to her room why don't you spend the night with me? Susan had retrieved my pajamas they were folded neatly upon the bed I changed in the bathroom and I climbed into her bed, I was baffled because I felt guilty, I had taken someone's life, Chris's existence had ended because of me, How could I get past this? Grand whispered Kimberly you must ask God to forgive you and you must forgive yourself, I quietly said, Yes but I'm not sorry that he is dead I'm just sorry that I had a hand in his demise I will never ever get over this, it happened so fast, maybe I could have done something else maybe…. Grand replied you must sleep now; we will figure out how to handle this tomorrow not now! Shaking my head gently in agreement and I closed my eyes. Sleep wasn't far away and I thank God for that. I was awaken by Grand's sweet soprano I sat up in the bed and glanced around she said good morning Kimberly, I jumped out of bed and said Good Morning Grandma she smiled blissfully at me and before she could talk I skipped out and went into my humble abode at least it use to be that, I closed the door and I glanced at the floor where Chris body had been the carpet marks were still there I refused to wallow in my grief I felt more alive after my shower in mere minutes I was dressed. Susan was at my door about to knock so she kept up the façade with her knuckle gently tapping my nose I clucked her on her nose going in search of my breakfast I tried to no avail to drag the breakfast but Grand quickly saw through my ruse she said let's go girls standing at the front with our backpacks I saw Mom in the front seat peering at me we got in Susan plugged in her earbuds somehow she knew Mom's agenda, Kimberly this too will pass, I said sure, Mom I secretly harbored some anger for her because she had known what he was about and she had done nothing to stop it so yes I was mad and I had every right to be, turning to gaze out the window that's when I saw a shadow in the tree line could it be Chris yes of course it could? My nerves were raffed,, oh my God, was this nightmare ever going to end that's when I made the decision to end my life, Grand came out of the house with a stern look upon her face she got in the car the moment was awkward for me she spoke to me I acknowledge her with a huge grin because I had found a way out of this situation now I know you are saying that's not the way to handle it but remember this is my way and I am going to handle it a huge brick seemed to be lifted off of my shoulders and I felt euphoria swept over my entire being when I got out and walked in the school a haze descended walking through the hallways everyone eyes were on my person they must know I've been raped, degraded my innocence discarded like a piece of trash It didn't register to me that I was an attractive young lady and I carried myself with a grace that I was born with no I had clarity only chaos not paying any attention I walked directly into Carmen and Nicole the impact of her shove sent me backwards a sharp pain radiated in my back I laid there for a minute without saying anything then I rolled over and gathered all my things they were expecting to get a rise out of me but none was forthcoming lesbo Carmen said I walked calmly by them like they weren't even there I had to find April because I needed a friendly face I turned the corner and she grabbed me and hugged me asking me if I was alright I assured her that I was ok she glanced deeply in my eyes and asked Kimberly has something happened I hesitated for a second then I returned her look and said Girl you know I'm fine! She released me but I could tell she didn't believe me I said jovially we mustn't be late this kid must on time, she glanced at me and said I know right retrieving our books we arrived in the class just as the bell rang no I don't recall much about that day the only thing that mattered to me was spending time with my very best friend April I spoke when spoken to I laughed at the appropriate times but I was holding on by a thread trust me a very thin thread soon the day was over before we parted ways I hugged her with a virtuosity, she stepped back and said Kim I.... I interrupted her and said see you tomorrow I wanted to reveal to her my true and deepest feeling but if I did I was aware she would figure it out and I couldn't allow that I walked out of the school but before I did I went over to the giant wolf that adorned our cafeteria and I whispered bye old friend in my mind I could hear the remnants of him crying softly for me with a strange melancholy smile I walked outside and saw our vehicle and jumped in Grand, Mom and Susan turned and said hi Kimberly how was day? Grand asked me it was so like her, smiling I said I had a great day! Other than dealing with Carmen and her entourage it was indeed a great day! Grand said I'm not cooking today so you can have whatever you want within reason she added Susan and I both glanced at each other and said Pizza, Grand said Pizza hut it is! We drove home chatting amicably with each other Mom even joined in, several times Grand glanced at me in the rearview but I only sent her happiness and I guess in some weird way I was, Grand ordered the pizza while we did our homework the pizza arrived piping hot we gathered at the table Grand said the blessing we dove in and it was good she ordered pineapple and Canadian bacon, pepperoni, three cheese, we were ravenous plenty of ribbing and laughter to go around we sat there long after there long after the pizza was gone, Mom asked Susan why don't you sleep with me tonight she jumped at the chance she ran off to gather her things while I hugged Grand and Mom bidding them goodnight stopping at the door to say I love you guys! They both said I love you Kimberly finally escaping to my room I locked the door I quickly penned my letters one for Mom, Grand, Susan, and April I would wait until everyone went to bed I showered I had bought some pull-ups so that wouldn't be a mess to clean up I pulled the package out of the back of the closet I opened it and pulled one out I took off my robe and I put on a pair of my favorite pajamas I laid on the bed waiting thoughts were swirling around in my mind everywhere I went people would think I asked for this to happen, they would ridicule me, judge me without knowing the full story, I felt so ashamed I had had a bright future planned but now I only had despair and loathing I prayed that God would forgive me but you must always ask him to forgive after you commit an offense I watched IG and some of my favorite videos and listened to music the last thing I did was pray reading the bible I read all of PSALMS it being one of my favorite soon the house settled and it started to rain now remember at the beginning of my story I hung myself now that you know why I did this maybe you will understand why there was no there was no other option my body swayed back and forth the pain was excruciating if someone tell you it is instant they are lying, I faded in and out consciousness why was it taking so damn long ,I needed for it to be over with already a dead chill came over my body I heard a loud sound my mind couldn't register that it was the beam that supported this room I opened my eyes for the last time and the air stirred all around me standing directly in front of me was the biggest most magnificent Angel he was so eminence his hair was long to his shoulders he chest held a gold breast plate and in his hand he held a gold gleaming sword it was also gold the brightest gold I had ever seen he stared at me like you would do to a disobedient child but his entire being was love, it was the love of our heavenly father no we may not deserve it but he loves us just the same, remember no one will ever love you the way that he does! he lifted his sword and beams started to expanse and then break all at once the beam gave away and I hit the floor with a huge thump I opened my eyes he was still standing there and he said Death is final?, there is no coming back! life maybe hard but you can withstand anything with our heavenly father's help he smiled at me and disappeared. gasping for air I shakily removed the noose from around my neck the rain had turned into full-fledged thunder storm and I removed all the debris from my room I swept my floor and then I came back in and sat on the bed I stared at the beam it looked strong enough to support me why hadn't? well I can tell you why, it wasn't my time sometimes we can do things or be involved in circumstances that will change the plan that God has for us I dropped to my knees my arms outstretched and I cried like a baby more than anything I cried and thanked God that I hadn't succeeded, times may be tough but we are made up of some very tough material you and I mean God engineered us this way life is fleeting so cherish it and never take a step without talking to someone first. I have no idea how long I cried and prayed but I thank him that he gave a second chance but somewhere near the ravine a shadowy figure lay still as stone then his eyes opened..........

My nightmare was far from over!